Storm paused sadly. "Bronwen must have been mad to give up so much for your father."

"You, of course, will be more sensible when you fall in love."

"You bet," she replied vehemently.

"You talk like a young virgin who has yet to experience passion," Carlo said.

"I don't have to live the experience. Bronwen did it for me."

"Nobody can ever do that. You have to step into the water yourself."

He pulled her into his arms, and she felt herself drowning in the burning power of his masculinity. She was still clinging to him as he held her at arm's length, a smile curving his lips.

"I'm going to possess you, Storm, just as she possessed my father."

SANDRA CLARK was born in Yorkshire. After leaving university she had several jobs, including running an art gallery, a guest house and a boutique. In addition to romance writing she has written several plays for theater and television. To relax she turns to sailing, reading and interior decorating, and she helps out at a children's nursery whenever she can. The author now lives in York with her two teenage children.

Books by Sandra Clark

HARLEQUIN PRESENTS

514—THE WOLF MAN

HARLEQUIN ROMANCE

2533—MOONLIGHT ENOUGH
2569—STORMY WEATHER
2780—A FOOL TO SAY YES

SANDRA
CLARK

too dangerous to love

Harlequin Books

TORONTO • NEW YORK • LONDON
AMSTERDAM • PARIS • SYDNEY • HAMBURG
STOCKHOLM • ATHENS • TOKYO • MILAN

Harlequin Presents first edition April 1987
ISBN 0-373-10968-7

Original hardcover edition published in 1986
by Mills & Boon Limited

Printed in U.S.A.

CHAPTER ONE

THE unexpected sound of a car purring into the courtyard brought Storm's head jerking up sharply, and a puzzled frown appeared on her small heart-shaped face. Everyone had already left and there were no appointments in the book for the rest of the week. Curious, she went to the window and gazed down into the cobbled courtyard.

Her expression changed to one of amazement when she saw a beige and silver Rolls drawing up beneath the window of the studio. Even as she watched, it stopped, and a man was already uncoiling from within, though all she could see was the top of a very dark head and the long length of his legs as he emerged.

With a nonchalance unexpected in a stranger, he climbed out of the car and strolled over towards the house as if, she thought, pursing her lips, he visited small fifteenth-century Welsh tower houses every day of his life. Most people gave the place a cursory glance at least.

Scowling, she watched him approach the main door and then, instead of ringing the bell, he tried the handle, pushed it and, without even pausing, marched in over the threshold.

'Well, of all the cheek!' Flinging her drawing pen on to the work bench, she raced across the studio to the stone stairs that led down into the yard. She had to pass next to the stranger's car, and its sheer size and opulence made her painfully conscious of her dishevelled appearance.

It had been a long and busy day. Her smock was streaked with coloured dyes and there was a smudge of drawing-ink across one cheek, while her long, straight-as-silk Titian hair was pulled back functionally in a plain elastic band. Not the way she wished to present herself to a client, but there was no time now to improve matters. The man was already inside the house.

As she reached the door she was aware of how cross she felt. Clients didn't usually go strolling about the place without a by-your-leave. They made proper appointments and waited for someone to fetch them up to Fferllys House in a car. Nor did they turn up out of official work hours, as if she had nothing better to do than jump to their attention. She was only working late now because—well, because.

She flung the door open, expecting to find him hovering around in the lobby, but it was empty. Stifling a further gasp of annoyance at the realisation that he must be prowling round the kitchen—and that wouldn't bear close inspection at the moment—she cautiously pushed at the door. To her further astonishment there was still no sign of him.

Surely he can't have gone upstairs? she frowned to herself. A flicker of fear bound itself tightly around her at the ease with which her privacy was being invaded by a complete stranger, and a tall, powerful and very masculine one at that.

Taking her courage in both hands, she forced herself to ascend the stairs. There was just the one staircase, a narrow stone spiral leading to the upper rooms—to the sitting-room on the next floor and then beyond that to the three small rooms on the floor above where her own bedroom and what had been Bronwen's bedroom and studio were situated.

Undecided whether to call out, alerting him to her presence, or to creep up unawares, she began to ascend with caution. If he turned out to be a rather well-heeled gentleman burglar, she would prefer to make a silent reconnoitre so that she could get away to ring for the police without him knowing. Now she found she was trembling violently, all at once aware of how isolated the house was, the nearest source of help being a good half-mile away in the village, well out of earshot.

Emerging soundlessly on to the tiny stone-flagged landing, she pushed open the sitting-room door and peered cautiously inside. As before, the room was empty. He seemed to have vanished! But she was positive she had seen him enter the house. Cursing under her breath, she gripped the brass stair-rail. There was no doubt about it—he must have actually gone up to the bedrooms!

A surge of anger sweeping away her fear, she sprinted two-at-a-time up the stairs. The three doors gaped open as if he had taken a brief look into each room before choosing which one to inspect more fully. She could see easily into the two small bedrooms, and as they were empty it could mean only one thing. Steeling herself for what could now only become a confrontation, she pushed open the door of Bronwen's studio and marched in.

The man was bending over her aunt's work table beneath the window when he heard the door open and she had the fleeting satisfaction of seeing a look of incredulity cross his face as he swung round to face her.

'Caught in the act!' she cried triumphantly. 'What the hell do you think you're doing in here?'

She strode across the room with her heart hammering behind her ribs, trying to look as intimidating as possible. It was like water off a duck's back though—and no wonder. If it came to a physical contest he would win hands down, she recognised with a quickly stifled shiver, for he was even more powerfully built than that first glimpse from the studio had allowed, and despite the impeccable tailoring of his light grey suit, he had the appearance of an athlete in prime condition.

It gave him an ambiguous air, making him difficult to categorise, and the wild, dark, foreign look of his deeply-tanned skin and blue-black, rather long hair, added to the effect. There had never been any clients on the books who looked like this.

With a jolt like an electric charge she felt the impact of

intense blue eyes, their thick dark lashes only serving to emphasise the icy clarity of their unusual colour. They swept over her without warmth, skewering her to the spot so that the hot words that had already sprung to her lips trailed away and she felt her mouth open and close soundlessly like a fish gasping for air.

'And who *the hell* are you?' he asked in a voice whose timbre sent wriggles of emotion snaking up her body and exactly matched her own in insolence. Storm gaped, unable to think of a thing to say, before she managed to rally her wits.

'Don't you know this is a private house?' she stabbed out, deliberately ignoring his question. 'Do you usually go creeping around places that don't belong to you? You've got a confounded cheek. If you don't explain, and quickly, I shall call the police and have you removed.' She drew herself up to her full height of five feet two inches. Meeting his eyes was like standing in the path of an arctic gale but she glared up at him defiantly, determined not to drop her glance first.

Then he surprised her by giving a small, hard chuckle.

'You do look ridiculous, glowering up at me like that. Where's your mother?'

'My mother's dead,' she replied cuttingly before she could stop herself.

'I'm sorry to hear that,' he returned, his tone bland. 'What about your nanny then, the person with the unfortunate task of looking after you?'

'I am entirely capable of looking after myself, thank you.' Her chin rose. 'Now will you stop asking *me* questions and answer a few yourself. This is private property and I want you to explain yourself or get out!'

'Come off it, sweetness,' he replied, unperturbed by her manner, 'I came inside in good faith, and when I saw no one around I came up here expecting to find the grown-ups. I didn't realise I'd accidentally strayed into your nursery.' He must have heard her sharp intake of breath as she was about to give him a piece of her mind, for he went on, 'Don't worry. I'm not going to break up your pretty toys, but be a good girl and let someone know I'm here, will you?'

Storm felt an explosion of rage propel her towards him. 'You damned patronising devil! Now get out of my house, will you? Who the blazes do you think you are?' Her eyes travelled rapidly over the expensive suit in keeping with the Rolls parked casually aslant the cobbles in the yard outside, and came to rest on the darkly handsome face with dislike. Even his very cheekbones, high and prominent, seemed to provoke her with their cutting arrogance.

'How dare you come snooping in here?' she demanded hotly, beside herself with the sheer effrontery of the man. 'What right do you think you've got?'

He was unmoved. 'Every right.' He gave her a frosty up and down look that made her shiver. 'I now own the place—for what it's worth.' He gave a cruelly critical glance round the cluttered room. 'Now who the blazes do you think *you* are, little girl?'

Storm's mind reeled. With a strangled gasp she managed enough control to croak, 'But it can't be true! You're not . . .' She put a hand to her brow as if to focus properly. 'You're too young to be . . .'

Acutely conscious of how she must look in her work smock with the big patch pockets and the bands of dye staining it where she had leaned up against the edge of the dyeing tank, her long hair pulled back any-old-how and with smudges on her face, she felt a scarlet flush creep up the length of her body as his piercing appraisal took in all these details with no more trace of warmth than a rattlesnake. His glance seemed to strip her to the skin, leaving her without a thread of clothing for protection, and her cheeks pained her with the blood that rushed hectically towards them.

Putting both hands up to hide this betrayal of her

feelings she half-turned as if to run away but in two strides he was beside her; she flinched as a strong brown hand gripped her by the arms and tried to pull her hands away from her face.

'What's the matter? Aren't you going to answer me?' Unblinking eyes blazed down into hers and she stepped back as if to get out of his reach, but he simply increased the pressure of his grip and gave her a little shake for good measure. 'Who are you?' he demanded, freezing her with the raw impatience he was making no effort to conceal. 'I didn't know Bronwen had a daughter.'

'Of course she didn't!' She laughed mirthlessly. 'I'm Storm—Bronwen's niece. Now let go!'

He gave a muttered exclamation and slowly released her. 'Is there anywhere we can talk?' he demanded, giving a cursory and critical glance around the cluttered room with its single chair in front of the drawing board.

Humiliated by the thoughts that she guessed were going through his head during this brief examination, she turned towards the door. 'Let's go into the sitting-room. This was Bronwen's power-house.'

If his eyebrows quirked at her strange description of what must to him look like a kind of chaos, he didn't make any comment, and she was too shocked by his claim that he actually owned Fferllys to want to bother to explain just yet. 'This way,' she muttered. The doorway was narrow and she felt her skin flush as his suit-clad body brushed against her when she closed the door behind them.

It was such a sudden and violent response, unequivocally sexual in its overtone, that it threw her off-balance both physically and mentally and she had to clutch at the banister rail before descending. Her senses seemed to prickle with an awareness of the total maleness of him and she caught the faint, arousing, masculine scent of his body when he came close to her. There was something dangerous and rawly sexual about him that made any normal proximity seem like an act of blatant intimacy; she was appalled at the diabolical ease with which her imagination was flooded with images of his unclothed body. But he allowed her no time to dwell on such fantasies, for his uncompromising glance briefly swept the sitting-room before coming to rest on her flushed face in a cool, casual appraisal that made her shudder inwardly.

His blue eyes travelled lingeringly over the rest of her body and a mocking smile came into them, curving the wide, straight mouth without humour. He seemed to exude a ruthless confidence in every move he made, causing her to watch him closely.

'It's all going to need a hell of a lot of work before it can be put on the market. She sure didn't care, did she?' His eyes glittered coldly as they registered her sharp intake of breath. 'What's the matter? Did you expect to go on living here for free as *she* did?' He turned away before she could bring some order to her jumbled thoughts. 'Tough on you,' he added brutally over his shoulder. 'Now, what about a drink?' He swung back to subject her again to the laser-bright blue eyes. 'I've flown three thousand miles and driven non-stop from Heathrow. If this is the best in hospitality Fferllys can provide I give you zero out of a hundred.'

Scorched by the contempt in his voice, Storm struggled to regain some vestige of self-possession. 'If it's light refreshment you require, I'm sure the inn in the village will be able to supply your needs,' she clipped. 'I don't keep open house for every passing stranger and although you may own Fferllys—a point, I might suggest, that has yet to be proved—you by no means own everything in it!' Her chin had risen and she forced herself to look him squarely in the eye.

As before, he laughed humourlessly at her defiance, and with a shudder she realised that, whatever she said, the look in his enigmatic blue eyes was that of a man who expected to get his own way in everything. It took all her self-control to hold his gaze.

When he replied his voice was so soft she at first missed the threat underlying the words; the mocking smile playing around his wide, sensual mouth lulled her into believing he was offering some kind of olive branch, until their full import hit her with a sickening impact.

'What I want, I get,' he told her with soft menace. 'And if I decide I want anything in Fferllys,' he paused significantly, 'make no mistake, I'll have it . . . and that, my sweet innocent, includes you. Now,' his tone changed, 'are you going to get me a drink, or do I have to rummage through the place myself?'

With a small gasp halfway between anger and fear, she swivelled towards the door.

While she was busy in the kitchen her mind was working overtime. It raced back to that dreadful night when everything had changed forever. The night when, five long weeks ago, the river had burst its banks, sweeping away her old life in the tragedy that heralded the new. Afterwards, sitting in David's office to hear the reading of the will, she had received the first intimation of trouble.

'But David, is that all?' She regarded her aunt's solicitor with troubled eyes as he finished reading the will and, without looking at her, began to finger the documents on his desk for a moment as if weighing one word against another.

'Well?' she insisted, becoming aware of a growing throb of anxiety at the rather embarrassed expression in David Marshall's face. She knew him well and whenever she came down from Fferllys they would have lunch together. His father, senior partner in the family firm, had been a confidant of Aunt Bronwen for years. He was near retirement age now and David was slowly building a reputation for himself as the heir apparent. She expected him to be frank with her, given their long-standing friendship, but now he was looking almost shifty.

'Sorry about this, Storm, but we all know how eccentric your Aunt Bronwen was, and she——'

'Not eccentric,' Storm replied defensively, 'artistic and very talented.'

David gave a slight shrug. 'Of course.' He was a young man with his feet very firmly planted on the ground, the artistic temperament that had made Bronwen leave a mere scrap of a will on one of those forms obtainable in any stationery store irritated him in a way he couldn't explain even to Storm. 'The fact of the matter is, Storm, that, unknown to any of us, your aunt did not actually own Fferllys. Now I know this must be a terrible shock——' he held up a hand as she gave a snort and seemed about to interrupt again, 'but we mustn't jump to any conclusions at this stage. Things may not be as bad as they seem.'

'But she *must* own it,' she burst out.

'I'm afraid not.' He shook his head.

'Then who the devil does?' she demanded, irritated by his methodical manner.

He gave an apologetic little cough. 'I took the liberty of checking through some papers your aunt lodged with Father some years ago——' He paused.

Storm knew the answer even before he spoke. 'Your aunt's—er—friend Griff Llewellyn is—er—the actual owner,' he admitted.

'Friend? Her ex-lover, you mean,' corrected Storm brutally. 'Let's not beat about the bush, David.' She pursed her lips. 'I must say it's a bit of a shock. I didn't have him down in my book as a benefactor. A philanderer, a plunderer of Bronwen's good will and generosity, her captor even——' she laughed shakily, 'but not a man to give anything away. A taker, that man, that's what *he* is——'

Ignoring all this, David clasped his hands together and leaned towards her over the mounds of documents. 'I have to ask you if you know his present address, Storm—I didn't realise you knew about their relationship.' He cleared his throat apologetically. 'Father mentioned him in passing when the question of ownership came up——'

'I'm not a child, David.' Her face softened for a moment. 'I'm old enough at twenty to know about extra-marital sex.' Her eyes gleamed mischievously as she saw she had embarrassed him by her outspokenness. He had held her hand once, recently, as they walked from a restaurant he had taken her to, and she had been amazed at the air of burning his boats he had assumed as he did so.

'And no,' she added, 'I don't know his address, though I dare say it may be among Bronwen's things.' Her face saddened. 'I haven't had the heart to go through anything yet.' Suddenly her violet eyes sheened with tears. Mere days had elapsed since Bronwen's funeral and Storm was still in a state of shock.

David got up and went to a cabinet. He poured a small glass of brandy and brought it round the desk towards her. 'Gosh, Storm, I know this is all such a damned awful mess, but you can rely on Dad and me, you know. You mustn't worry about a thing.'

His very niceness brought tears stinging to her eyes. She tried to dash them away but they fell in an angry, scalding stream all over her face and she saw them plop in large drops on to the shiny patent leather of her handbag without being able to stop them.

David put one hand awkwardly on her shoulder and as if unused to any show of emotion patted her once or twice without speaking.

'I'm sorry, David,' she murmured tightly, 'I didn't mean to break down. It's just the shock really.'

'It was a devil of a way to—you know. Drowning like that. I'm sure it was quick, Storm.' He patted her again and with an effort she managed to bottle up her tears.

'Bloody bridge,' she muttered tearfully. 'Still,' she

straightened her back, 'no use crying, is it? But what shall I do now, David?' She raised wide violet eyes helplessly to his.

'Leave it all to us. If you can get that address to me when and if you find it, we'll contact Llewellyn and let him know what's happened. I feel sure,' he added, 'that given the circumstances he'll be only too happy to let things go on as they have done. I don't imagine he's short of a bob or two and he hasn't left South America for donkey's years. The tower house is no use to him, is it? I can't see that it'd be any skin off his nose to let you go on living there, though I must say, it must be a devil of a place to run.'

Storm contemplated the drop of brandy remaining in the glass, then gulped it down before rising to her feet. 'I have no choice, David. I must stay there to run our business—*my* business,' she corrected, 'or at least, 'she bit her lip, 'I'll have to stay until I can relocate the studio and print workshop. The trouble is—where?' Her small heart-shaped face was pale.

'I'm sure it won't come to that.' He began to shepherd her towards the door. 'We'll talk again when we find out what Griff Llewellyn's intentions are.' His tone changed. 'I can't tempt you to a spot of lunch, can I?'

'Thank you, but no. I must get back.' She was mildly amused at the thought of David tempting her to anything. 'We've got a special commission on,' she explained, 'and things are a bit hectic—I could do with thirty-six hours in the day, not twenty-four.'

'Yes—keep yourself busy,' he agreed, rather patronisingly she thought, as if the fabric design business she was now in sole charge of was just a minor hobby. He was gazing at her steadily with his calm grey eyes and with an awkward dipping movement of his head he planted a light kiss on her forehead. 'I'll try and drive out to see you as soon as I can.'

With a squeeze of her shoulder he let her go and she

made her way back down the narrow stairs to the street. It was market day, but she was scarcely aware of the crowds of farmers and housewives who bustled about the narrow streets. She had expected the reading of the will to be a mere formality, though if she had really paid attention when David rang her to arrange a meeting, she would have recognised the note of worry in his voice.

As Bronwen's niece and only living relative she had expected Fferllys to become hers. In fact, it had never even occurred to her to consider the matter. Bronwen was only fifty, fit and energetic, and the prospect of her death had never really entered Storm's head. But for a rainy night—with a cloudburst typical in its suddenness of this part of central Wales—the wooden bridge over a usually placid river in the mountains would not have been swept away in the sudden violent flood of water that had burst the river banks. Bronwen, having dined with friends further down the valley, had set off to drive back to Fferllys in the dark. Her headlamps must have failed to pick out the treacherous black flood that had cut the winding mountain road in two, and she must have driven on to what was left of the bridge before realising that its central support had been swept away. A dawn search-party had discovered the little blue car upside down in the mud at the bottom of the river some five hundred yards downstream. Bronwen was still at the wheel.

Storm shuddered to recall the sleepless night through which she had kept a vigil, expecting at any minute to see the headlamps of the car bravely approaching across the mountain-side through torrents of rain. Throughout that long first morning, as she had waited for the waters to recede so that she could confirm the horror of what had happened for herself, she had come face to face with the harrowing realisation that she was now completely alone in the world.

It was worse, now, than the time when her own mother had died, for she had been ill a long time and Storm herself had been only eight and there had been relatives to comfort the small child she had been then. And when her father was killed by terrorists in the Middle East five years later, it had been the logical outcome of the sort of life he had been leading as a war correspondent, forever first in the trouble spots of the world, with a sense of irresponsibility towards his own life that caused Bronwen, his sister, to throw up her hands in despair.

Storm had been living with Bronwen during the school holidays at this time and outwardly her life had scarcely changed. Only happy memories of her swashbuckling father remained, and the grief had never been without its overtones that his life had been well-lived. That same element of never compromising with fate applied to Bronwen too, though on the surface her life had been quite different. More inward-looking and serene, she had been the artistic one of the two and had managed to make a name for herself as a fabric designer, hand-printing on the finest silks and voiles to special commissions from private clients and small, exclusive fashion houses. Her reputation guaranteed a good though not lavish income for herself and her brother's child. She had never married.

It was some three weeks later that Storm was able to hand over Griff Llewellyn's South American address to David Marshall. It had taken that long to sift through the drawers of correspondence and folios of drawings, the boxes of photographs, diaries and postcards that crammed the tower room Bronwen had used as a studio where her design concepts were brewed.

Storm had always respected her aunt's privacy with regard to her studio and she was reluctant even now to do more than riffle the surface, looking for references to Griff Llewellyn, leaving the disposal of its contents for some painless time in the distant future. Bronwen had been a hoarder and there were many mementoes. Storm had had the heart-wrenching task of sifting through several drawers of letters from him that had accumulated over the years of their connection. She hesitated to use the word 'affair', for, despite her antipathy to the man who, she believed, had heartlessly seduced and abandoned Bronwen and yet, through thousands of miles, had somehow managed to keep her spirited and beautiful aunt in thrall to his charm to the very end, she was aware that for Bronwen at least it had been no mere sordid triangle with her aunt cast in the role of 'the other woman'. Its longevity was an indication of the depth of the relationship—at least for one of the participants.

At first it had looked to Storm as if Griff Llewellyn had never felt inclined to disrupt his safe, rich marriage for Bronwen's sake—and Storm had always resented this on her aunt's behalf even while it clashed with her own idea of what a true marriage should be. But in the end she had come to accept, as Bronwen herself seemed to accept, that the love she and Griff shared was too strong to be hidden, a natural force that was simply *there,* whether they were apart or together. Yet now she began to wonder whether Llewellyn's interest in Bronwen was because he owned the place she lived in.

Another two weeks had passed since she had dropped the scrap of paper with the rather grandiose-sounding address in Brazil on to David's desk with a sense of somehow sealing her own fate. Since then there had been no reaction.

That morning, as she had gone down into the kitchen to make herself a cup of coffee, the four women she employed were chatting amiably as they put on their hats and coats ready to go home.

Originally her aunt's loyal helpers from the early days of the business, they were her team now. Reassuringly they had transferred their loyalty to Storm, for as Megan, a widow with two teenagers to fend for, had so cogently observed, where else could they find work these days that lived up to what most of them had been used to for the last twenty years? They were craftswomen with skills that had been polished by use.

'Can you see us behind the cash desks of supermarkets, or scrubbing floors, chick? Don't be dull. We'll stay with you as long as you want us, God bless you.'

Storm was secretly moved to tears when she realised that Megan, her seventeen-year-old daughter Luce, and the two older women, Gwyneth and Phyllis, were going to stand by her, and though the older ones clucked over her like mother hens these days, in matters of company policy they were as eager to take her lead as they had once upon a time taken Bronwen's.

'Cheer up, pet,' Phyllis exclaimed when she caught sight of Storm's face behind her in the mirror. She had swung round with her hands still busy with the knot of her headscarf. 'That silk order's well on schedule.'

Storm laughed, regretting that she wore her anxiety written so visibly on her face. 'You know me,' she joked. 'Until I see it safely in the hands of the carriers my diet's going to be finger-nails!' In fact her nails were beautiful, but everyone laughed and she was relieved when they didn't probe further. The silk order was nothing to worry about. It was something far bigger than one order that bothered her, for every day brought them inexorably closer to that big question of whether the company would be allowed to survive or not. Everyone knew there were problems over the ownership of Fferllys. The news had hit them with as much force as it had hit Storm. But it was different for her, she had the responsibility of making it work out for everyone else.

When they had all gone, she had made her way back to the studio where she was working on some sketches for an order for material for a ball gown from one of her London clients. She remembered how she had tried to push her anxiety to one side as she settled down to work at the intricate detail of the design and how her thoughts had ranged around and around, hopelessly trapped until the one major question could be answered. Then had come the sound of the car entering the courtyard, purring with a sound like an insidious portent of doom.

Now her body burned with the humiliation of discovering that the cold, domineering male in the room upstairs was the owner of Fferllys—her aunt's ex-lover, if he was to be believed, and the man who now held the power to make or break her.

CHAPTER TWO

WITH an effort Storm made herself check the tray, grimacing when she realised that such was her state of mind she had forgotten the coffee pot. Scowling, she placed it next to the pretty china cups, part of a set Bronwen had bought years ago. She had barely been able to control her shaking fingers as she forced herself to go about the humiliating task of preparing a drink for him, and she was furious with herself for reacting so violently. What was the matter with her, for heaven's sake? She scolded herself as she balanced the tray on one hand in order to negotiate the kitchen door. She wasn't sixteen any longer. She had met plenty of sexy, handsome men in her life, but none of them had affected her in the way he had just done. No wonder Bronwen had been so smitten all these years.

Yet there was something that was not quite right. It had niggled away at her ever since she had come face to face with him—and it wasn't just the devastating effect of his blatant sex appeal, it was something else . . . he was so young, surely not more than thirty, thirty-two? She had imagined Griff to be around the same age as her aunt—his literary reputation just didn't fit a younger man. Did it mean that Griff had sold the tower house to this younger and more ruthless specimen without letting Bronwen know? And if so, who was he? The unmistakable air of foreignness was belied by his cut-glass English accent, yet he seemed to know all about Griff and admitted to having just flown three thousand miles, which must surely mean he had come straight from South America.

With such questions running riot amongst the turbulent emotions he had aroused, she began to climb back up the spiral stairs towards the sitting-room.

When she came in he was sprawled in one of the sagging chintz-covered armchairs, very much at home, she noted, his eyes pin-pointing her wherever she moved.

'You're not Griff Llewellyn, are you?' she forced herself to ask, setting the tray down carefully between them.

'Here's my card.' He leaned across the round oak table and held out a small white card between his fingers as a token of conventional behaviour that seemed unexpected coming from such a ruthlessly arrogant man.

She took it with a murmured thanks, painfully conscious of the brief contact of their skin as she did so. Her eyes flicked over the neat black italic script and widened involuntarily.

'Carlo Llewellyn . . . you're—you must be Griff's *son?*' she exclaimed. Everything fell into place. The dark gypsy looks would come from his mother—a Brazilian heiress—the blue eyes, from Griff himself.

'Is that proof enough that I own Fferllys? If not I can get you a copy of the Deeds——'

'I'm sure my solicitor will expect that——'

'But this will suffice for the time being, I hope?' His cold formality made her stiffen with apprehension. Everything he said was like the thrust of a rapier, designed to draw blood.

She nodded, 'I suppose it'll have to do for now.'

From his gleaming white shirt with the elegant width of cuff showing under the soft wool of his hand-stitched suit to the car outside, he exuded wealth, power and authority. It was a combination that made Storm bristle with fear. Why did he have to be so formidable? she asked herself. She knew they were in for a battle, every sign pointed to it, but it was going to be an unfair handicap to have to face up to such an arrogantly confident opponent by herself.

As he ate she longed to ask him a million questions, most of all whether he really intended to put Fferllys on the market, but she schooled herself to watch and wait. If she was going to fight him she must know her enemy as well as she knew herself. He began to bite into a slice of cake and chew on it with what seemed like deliberate slowness, as if determined to undermine her confidence right from the start. The bright glance met hers accusingly as he replaced his coffee cup in its saucer.

'Where did she keep everything?' he asked lazily.

Storm's eyes widened in puzzlement.

'Bronwen,' he elucidated with impatience. The harsh tone he gave to his utterance of her aunt's name made the hair on the back of her neck prickle alarmingly. It was as if he hated her. Yet why should he? She frowned slightly.

'You must mean the printing equipment——' she began, but he shook his dark head with irritation.

'Not her hobby materials—no. I don't imagine they cost Father more than a few hundred pounds. I mean the jewellery, the presents, the furs.' He gave her a withering look. 'I've come to reclaim what he was fool enough to give away.'

Storm looked at him as if he was suddenly speaking a foreign language. In fact she couldn't have been more confused if he had broken into the Welsh or the Spanish he no doubt also spoke in that alarmingly beautiful voice.

'Don't look at me as if you don't know what the hell I'm talking about,' he snarled softly. 'You know damn well what I mean.'

'I'm sorry——' She straightened. 'I *don't* know what you mean.'

'How long are we going to go on fencing with each other like this?' he demanded.

'For as long as it takes you to come clean about your intentions,' she declared, before she could bite the words back.

He gave her the benefit of a brief, sardonic smile, his full lips drawing back rapaciously as he said, 'I thought I'd made myself perfectly clear on that score. As soon as I've drunk this excellent coffee and eaten a slice of the home-made cake you've so kindly provided you're going to show me round Fferllys so that I can get an idea of what needs to be done before I can put it up for sale. Is that clear enough?

'You can't!' she gasped weakly, half-rising. 'You can't just march in here and sell my home from under my feet!' Her feelings spilled over. 'There must be laws, sitting tenants must have rights—you can't do it! I—I won't let you . . . You'll never get away with it!'

None of this was what she had intended to say but her worries seemed to burst through any natural restraint, revealing all her worst fears. His cold blue eyes watched her without expression and with as little compassion as if she had been an insect underfoot.

I don't know the details of the law over here, but I very much doubt whether you could be regarded as a bona fide tenant,' he replied impatiently. 'Have you anything in writing?'

'Of course not!'

'Of course not,' he agreed ironically.

'What does *that* mean?' Stung by his scathing tones, she glowered at him from across the table. At that moment she felt she would like nothing better than to hit him. He looked so sure of himself. He was insufferable.

'What does it mean? It means, dear child, that a man who keeps a mistress is likely to be so besotted he'll forgo all the usual business conventions that are designed to safeguard his property, and, if he's as unbusinesslike as my father, rest his soul, he'll dig deep in his pocket to provide whatever the pretty lady desires without record or receipt. And in this case it seems she desired a rather pleasant medieval castle——'

'Tower house,' she corrected automatically. 'But it wasn't——'

'I bow to your superior knowledge,' he went on without letting her finish. 'You've no doubt been living here long enough rent free to know the difference. Now, what I suggest——'

'Just wait a moment. You can't throw all that at me and expect me to go along with it——'

'I've certainly no intention of explaining anything further. My time is short.' He placed his empty plate on the table and rose to his full height. 'And whether you want to go along with it or not is irrelevant. You have no choice. Now, come along, show me the rest of my property.'

Storm pulled herself jerkily to her feet in a spasm of anger that brought her up closer than she had anticipated and she recoiled from the touch of the hard muscled body, confusedly aware of the dangers of such proximity. She stepped back until she found the wooden chair she had been sitting on digging into the back of her legs. It made her feel trapped. Responding like any cornered animal she lashed out as best she could.

'I've no damned intention of showing you anything!' she cried hoarsely. 'And until you go away and come back with a copy of the Deeds, and give me fair warning that you want an appointment to see the place at a time convenient to me, you can whistle! Now get out! That's my last word!' She would get David to come over, she thought feverishly. There was no way she was going to make herself face such a man alone once more. She was furious that she should have demonstrated just how vulnerable she really was, but her outburst had failed miserably.

'You can't seriously expect me to turn around, meek as a lamb, and go away again?' His eyes crinkled in amusement and his mirthless laugh sent a chill scudding up her body. 'Another thing you ought to learn is never to make warning noises unless you can back them up with deeds.' He moved closer. 'I think you've just played your last card.'

'W—What do you mean?' she stammered, her voice dropping to a frightened whisper as she became vibrantly conscious of the totally male power closing in on her.

'You've warned me off twice now, and both times I've refused, so what happens next?' His voice vibrated huskily and his lips hovered just within sight above her head. The cruel twist to his mouth taunted her as he brought his head closer and she tried vainly to tear her eyes away, but some strength in him kept her glance in thrall. She gave an involuntary shudder. 'Is this what kept Bronwen under Griff's spell all those years?' she demanded stoically, fighting in vain against the power that threatened her judgment.

His eyes darkened in hostility. 'Don't play games with me, Storm. That's not how it was and you know it.' He ran one finger in a provoking caress down the side of her face. 'Do you look like her? Did she use her treacherous violet eyes to ensnare my father and hold him all these years as you're trying to do to me?'

Storm's mouth had gone dry at his touch, making it impossible to reply and she felt with as little surprise as if it had been a dream, the strong-boned fingers slide down her arms, circling her wrists, biting into her tender flesh as panic coiled and exploded inside her and she felt his body grazing hers along its slim length.

'I thought you were threatening to throw me out?' he murmured against her ear. He pinned her arms effortlessly behind her back with one hand while the other slid up into her hair, loosening the long coils from the restraining band, and tightening into it until her head tilted back so that the slightest movement tugged hurtfully at her scalp. Taking his time he began to lower his dark head towards her, slowly, mercilessly, scrutinising her face as if trying to commit its expression to memory.

'Well, well,' he murmured, only a few inches away, 'so Bronwen's spirit lives on in the niece. How interesting this is going to be . . . But I think you ought to know from the beginning that I'm not made in the same soft mould as my father. I'm more than a match for you, Storm, however beguiling the façade that hides your conniving soul.'

Even if she could have gathered her wits to resist him, she was given no opportunity, for his mouth, softly sensual, came down on her own, forcing her lips to part, becoming hard and demanding as her own yielded helplessly at the onslaught of his touch. She made a muffled protest, but it was lost against the pressure of his mouth and she felt tears of helpless anger well up in her eyes, hating him with a bitterness that threatened to sweep everything else away. It was a kiss that desecrated everything that Bronwen had felt in her misguided way throughout the long years of her hapless love for Griff, and Storm felt shamed that Griff's son should be kissing her in the very house in which his father had kept Bronwen the prisoner of his heart for so long.

Despite her thoughts, she felt her body responding with shameful ardour to his embrace and she was filled with self-disgust that she should actually yield to such an intimate and loveless plundering without a semblance of a fight. He held her pliant body in his arms as he gave her flushed face an amused, analytical appraisal.

'Hot stuff, just as I expected,' he judged scornfully. 'She taught you well. I've no doubt the locals used to think of you and Bronwen as a couple of witches luring unsuspecting fools to your enchanted castle. What a pity your sway has to come to an end!'

Abruptly he let go of her wrists so that she staggered back, catching hold of the back of the chair to stop herself from falling.

'If you don't want to show me round, that's up to you. I'm going to have a look anyway. I'm intrigued to know what she spent a large part of our family fortune on—there's no evidence of much spending going into the furnishings.' His lips curled. 'Though I suppose that's to be expected. If I've got her right it would be more in her line to decorate herself, not her house. Where are the rooms full of clothes, where are the jewels kept?'

'There are no clothes or jewels, and if there were they wouldn't be yours. Everything Bronwen had she worked for.'

'There's work and work,' he observed cynically. 'And like you, I've no doubt she worked overtime.'

A fierce, piercing anger brought Storm's right hand up in a resounding slap that left an immediate red imprint on the side of his arrogant face.

Retribution was instant and unequivocal and she felt his arms snake round her waist, gripping her slender body helplessly against his own hard, muscled one as his lips came down savagely to imprison her own beneath the punishment of their grinding pressure.

The unfamiliar taste of blood was like metal on her lips as she strove to resist the harsh invasion of his tongue, her muffled protests failing to stop the growing passion with which his mouth ravaged her own in brutal possession. Breathless when he finally released her, she was painfully aware of the hostility of his glance as it swept over her flushed face.

'Don't make the mistake of expecting to get away with anything,' he intoned savagely, his eyes glittering with cold malice over her stricken face. Her eyes sheened as he swung his arrogant black head and made for the door. He pivoted when he reached it and looked back at her with an intense questioning glance that shivered her delicate frame.

From the first moment she had set eyes on him, his

looks, his harshness, who he was, had all come together to dash her hopes to pieces. Now it seemed futile to go on pitting herself against him. With a defiant toss of her long, burnished hair, that was now tumbling in disarray around her shoulders, she followed him out of the sitting-room on to the small landing, her whole body bruised and throbbing painfully at the insulting way he had forced her to succumb.

'Show me Bronwen's rooms,' he ordered. Without looking at him she led the way mutinously back up the staircase to the top where they had first encountered each other. He seemed surprised when she pushed open the door of the bedroom and he saw both how small it was and how bereft of possessions it seemed.

'Have you cleared her stuff out already?' he demanded harshly, going to stand with a proprietorial air in the middle and gazing critically at the old French armoire against one wall, the single four-poster with its pale lace counterpane and the single dark oak chest across one corner.

'She lived very simply,' replied Storm huskily. Tears crowded behind her eyes, for it seemed too painful to subject her aunt's few belongings to the scrutiny of this cold-hearted man. His black brows winged upwards with an expression of pure scepticism. Making his way to the armoire he tried to pull the heavy doors open. 'Key?' he demanded peremptorily, as if he expected her to claim it was lost.

'Certainly,' she replied frostily. 'There's nothing to hide. She must have put it away. I—I haven't opened any of her cupboards since——' She swallowed, unable to mention anything to do with that terrible night to this hateful man, and she was relieved when she had an excuse to turn away from the searching light of his eyes to conceal the evidence of her grief. Where he had pulled his hands roughly through her hair it had come free from its band and a long dark lock fell protectively over her face, concealing her expression from his scrutiny.

She reached into a small porcelain jug on the stone sill beneath the mullioned window and handed him the heavy ornate key before stepping back to watch as he fitted it in the lock and swung the doors wide.

She could tell at once that he was disappointed by what he saw. There were beautiful gowns of course, designed mostly by Bronwen herself, and he seemed to note these with satisfaction as if they proved a point, but what else he hoped to find was obviously not there, and he didn't bother to conceal his suspicions, shooting her a narrowed look that made her clench her fists in impotent rage.

'No fur coats, you see,' she couldn't help observing tartly, and was pleased to see her jibe get to him. Obviously he was a man who couldn't bear to be proved wrong. He made a cursory examination of the rest of the room, paying rather more attention to the jumbled contents of Bronwen's jewel box. Storm watched him run the assorted beads and baubles through his lean brown fingers. Bronwen had had a taste for the exotic, but apart from the intrinsic interest of some unusual pieces, most of them made up by friends in the jewel trade, there was nothing, she knew, that would impress a man with Carlo Llewellyn's obvious wealth.

Their eyes met over the glittering chaos in the velvet box, and Storm found it difficult to resist a small, cold smile that said as plainly as words, 'I told you so.' But Carlo was not to be put in the wrong.

'I don't believe this is all of it—anything valuable is presumably kept at the bank. I'll need her account numbers.'

'You'll have no such thing!' Defeated though she thought she was, her head rose with spirit. 'You don't own anything of hers, and neither did your father—though he damn well came near to trying to own *her*—keeping her a prisoner for life in this bloody place!'

Carlo slammed the jewel box down and came to tower

over her. 'What did you say?'

'You heard!' she responded rudely.

His hands came up powerfully to grip her by the shoulders, shaking her roughly, then abruptly letting her go as if he had thought better of it this time. He gave a glance at the thick gold watch on his wrist.

'What else is there on this floor?' he demanded abruptly.

'Only the room you've already seen—and my own bedroom.'

He stalked out ahead of her and crossed the landing and she followed, flinching as he gave her small, neat room a quick examination.

'They're like monks' cells,' he observed sardonically, 'or should I say nuns' cells?' he added in a harsher tone, 'though that's hardly appropriate in the circumstances.'

Storm smouldered but held her tongue. Let him think what he liked. As soon as he left she would ring David and together, surely, they could find a way out of this horrible situation Bronwen had unwittingly bequeathed.

By now he was back on the landing and trying to wrest open a small door in the wall.

'It's locked,' she told him curtly, 'and not for any nefarious reason, but merely because it leads up on to the roof. The key's downstairs in the kitchen if you want it.' Her tone made it clear that he would have to go and fetch it himself if he wanted to pry further.

'I'll have a look at the roof later when the surveyor comes,' he informed her coolly. 'Just show me the rest of your living quarters, then we'll call it a day. Where's the bathroom, by the way? You presumably *have* a bathroom?' He looked significantly at her still more dishevelled appearance.

'Inconveniently, it's on the floor below,' she replied evenly, without rising to the bait. She would not allow him to ruffle her any more.

'Yes, that's not very well planned. Why don't you open

this landing into the gallery?' He had noticed the bricked-up arch that would have once led into the rooms built on to the south wall of the house. It was a sort of curtain wall forming the fourth side of the rectangular building with the courtyard in the middle.

'They're just store rooms. It's always been separated from our domestic quarters like this. We've never needed to use that side of the building. I suppose the cost of making major alterations was always a deterrent,' she added. She scowled when she saw how quizzically amused he seemed. 'What have I said?'

'I can just imagine you two—nothing,' he replied, quickly correcting himself, but there was a wry smile on his face as he headed down the stairs to the ground floor that made him look almost human. When they reached the bottom he said seriously, 'I'd like you to tell me what we're looking at as we come to it.'

'Oh honestly, I'd have thought it was all obvious enough. Here's the kitchen on the ground floor of the round tower at the west end and there are the service rooms, pantry and buttery at the east end. There are a few small rooms, servants' quarters in the old days, I suppose——'

'"Kitchen and associated domestic offices" in the jargon of the estate agent, would you say?'

'If you like,' she replied sulkily.

'No, if *you* like, Storm,' he broke in, 'you're the one who's going to have to write it all up for me.'

'Me? Why me? It's bad enough having you snatch the place from under me without the humiliation of—it'd be like writing out my own death warrant,' she blurted helplessly.

'You're exaggerating of course, but you see,' he replied in a silky voice, 'that's exactly what I want to do—humiliate you. Somebody has to pay for the way Bronwen tried to break up my parents' marriage, for the way she humiliated my mother and for the way she tried to bleed Father dry. And as she's no longer with us, it'll have to be you.'

Her startled glance made him laugh maliciously. 'I've decided to revise my plans,' he went on blandly. 'I'm not going to throw you out just yet.' He paused. 'Instead I'm going to exact payment for all the wrongs done to us.'

'But it wasn't *my* fault that Bronwen and your father had an affair! She made the mistake of half-turning, as if to dismiss him.

'It wasn't *my* fault!' he mimicked savagely, grasping her by the shoulder again and swinging her round to face him. His eyes had darkened in a way which was becoming familiar. She took a shuddering step back, staring up at him speechlessly. 'And don't give me that wide-eyed innocent look. You've demonstrated clearly enough to me that you're exactly the same type as your aunt. You seem to imagine that by blinking those big beautiful eyes of yours you can soft-soap me into letting you live at Fferllys for nothing. Well, those days are over and you'd better believe it. What you want, you pay for. And, sweetheart, you're going to pay—with interest!' Carlo was shaking her violently but let her go so suddenly that she staggered back against the wall, jolting her shoulder so painfully that she had to stifle a cry.

He looked at her coldly for a moment, then added, 'Don't try to convince yourself that I'm the soft-hearted fool my father was. I saw what hell Bronwen created and I'm not going to let you get away scot-free.'

'None of this is true, Carlo,' she managed to cry in a strangled voice. 'Bronwen would never do anything to hurt anyone. Personally I think she was crazy to waste her life the way she did, longing for one man like the heroine in some novelette. Every day was spent in the hope that Griff would come back to her, that he would show he loved her as totally as she loved him. She wasn't after what she could get. She could have had everything—a husband, children—but she took nothing, except a place to live—a place she kept for him, for when he would eventually return——'

'And when was that wonderful day going to be, Storm?' His eyes bored into hers. 'It was to be the day Mother died. But she hasn't died. What she has had to endure is the pain and humiliation of her husband killing himself because of the death of his mistress!'

'No——'

'Yes, Storm. How else do you imagine I've inherited? Shall I tell you what else I got in his will—apart from this love nest,' he hissed. 'I'll tell you,' he went on inexorably. 'I've had the pleasure of inheriting all his unpublished writing, and you can guess who the dark lady of his fantasies turned out to be. This ideal woman, the one he would never name——' He gave a short bitter laugh. 'Critics assumed she was an invention, but she was no fiction.' He ran a hand through his sleek black hair. 'When I was a child my life was scarred by the fearful fights my parents used to have over some other woman. In the last few years they seemed to reach a truce. I thought it was all finished with this other——' He paused as if unsure what name to call her.

'With Bronwen, you mean?' she clipped, her own eyes hard.

'Yes—Bronwen. But how we were all deceived!' He laughed bitterly again and his lips curled in disgust. 'Father, the saint, with all his admirers—he has quite a literary reputation in South America——'

'And here too,' Storm remarked.

'Yes, well perhaps one day they should all know the truth——'

'What? That he loved two women? Or one, or six hundred? Does it matter now?'

'It matters to me. It matters to my pride that my mother should have had to suffer the humiliation—you weren't there to see the adoring students sitting at his feet as if pearls fell from his lips. But it was all a sham. His writings weren't the outpourings of some noble, spiritual love, they were the ramblings of a man besotted. He was possessed by Bronwen, and now I'm going to possess you, Storm, just as *she* possessed and corrupted him!'

He pulled her into his arm's and once again she felt the burning power of his masculinity eat into her will. With a spark of desperate longing she found herself clinging to him, letting his lips search out the soft, secret places of her mouth. With an abrupt movement of his dark head he forced her back, holding her at arm's length; a smile curved his lips and his eyes smouldered with the lust for revenge. 'I'm going to enjoy this, Storm,' he grated. 'How does it feel to know you're in my power? Does it frighten you to imagine what I might do?'

He ran a hand firmly and possessively down the supple length of her spine, then stepped back, letting her go abruptly and switching at once to a cold businesslike manner as if his kisses had meant less than nothing. Storm caught her breath with the sharpness of her gut reaction to this deliberate ploy.

'Show me the rest of the place,' he commanded, not looking at her. 'What are those buildings over there?'

He pointed to the workshops. Storm answered stiffly in a flat, emotionless voice, astonished at the ease with which he could switch off while, by contrast, her whole body still throbbed painfully from his touch. She began to walk blindly like an automaton across the yard. She had to make him see that he was wrong about Bronwen, that there was another side to the affair that he could know nothing about, but her mouth felt numbed, not only by the savagery of their physical contact, but as much by the feelings of helplessness that were welling up inside her. His power was overwhelming in its intensity and he seemed to shake her to the very foundations of her being.

'What do you mean, workshops?' he demanded as she began to unlock the doors.

'See for yourself,' she replied stiffly, running a hand through her hair and trying to clear her thoughts. It made her feel dead inside to stand in the brilliantly lit workshop and to know that however vital and successful it was in its way it was about to be destroyed by the will of this man. Whatever he said about not throwing her out just yet, there was no way he could make her stay so that he could exact payment for imagined wrongs. She was crying inside at the thought that all of Bronwen's life work, and her own too so far, was about to be destroyed because of this one man.

The heavy silence that seemed to be emanating from him made her dart a quick glance to where he was poking about amongst some silk-screens stacked against one wall.

'What goes on here?' He swivelled to look at her.

'The printing, as you can see,' she replied wearily.

'What printing? What are you talking about?'

She gaped at him helplessly.

'What printing? Who for? Who does it?' he insisted.

Her eyes were bleak. 'I do it, of course, with the help of my four workers.'

'What workers?'

'Women from the village down the valley. You must have come through it on the way up here.' She looked at him more closely. 'They've been with Bronwen ever since she first started the company.'

The expression on his face was pure puzzlement. 'Are you trying to tell me Bronwen ran a business from here?'

'I thought you knew. You seem to think you know everything that goes on here,' she couldn't help adding cuttingly.

His confusion made his usually arrogant face look suddenly more vulnerably attractive, and for a brief instant she caught a glimpse of the man he might be underneath the hatred. But his swaggering confidence took over at once as he completed his inspection of the premises with the cold, assessing eye of a man adding up the worth of his possessions. When he finished she expected some sarcastic comment about the state of the place. The immaculate grey suit he wore looked incongruous in such a place, with its dye-spattered floor, the jars of brushes, wood-shavings where someone had been making frames, the drying racks, the old blocks stained with dye, the big zinc tubs and the printing tables with their signs of continuous use. A streak of scarlet had stained the stone floor like a blood stain where someone had knocked over a can of dye, and to someone who didn't know what they were looking at it must have seemed a mess.

'And the room above?' Carlo had completed his inspection and come to stand in front of her with a thoughtful look in his eyes.

'That's the studio where the designs are drawn up.' She turned and led the way up the iron spiral that had been put in to connect the two floors without the necessity of walking outside again.

The studio was plain, simple and light. Cutting tools and waxing implements lay neatly on the shelves, and swatches of fabric samples glowed richly on the racks. He made straight for the drawing board where Storm had been working on a new design that afternoon and after a close inspection of it came back to where she leaned against the top of the stairs.

The veiled blue of his eyes deliberately told her nothing of what he was thinking and she forced herself to hold his glance without blinking. Casually he reached out and took one of her hands in his, spreading her fingers in his smoothly tanned palm so that she became acutely aware of the stains under her finger nails.

'Nothing Swarfega can't change,' she muttered defensively, raising her chin.

'Then I suggest you obtain some of this Swarfega and

use it. I'm not taking you out to dinner with hands like that.'

'You're not taking me out to dinner, full stop.'

'No?' His blue eyes mocked her and she felt his male power sweep over her. Her mouth went dry. His attention was so acute that he noticed her capitulation as it happened.

'Don't take more than half an hour. Can you do it?'

Eyes lowered, she gave a small, mutinous nod.

'Mind if I stay up here while you change?'

'It's all the same if I do mind, isn't it?' she retorted, then, catching sight of the humorous gleam in his eyes, she felt the tug of her own traitorous response in the half-smile that briefly lit her face.

'That's right,' he murmured, 'you're beginning to understand. You can't win and you'll only get hurt if you fight.'

Her heart-shaped face became taut, and she tried and failed to keep the hopeless note out of her voice when she replied deliberately, 'You don't have to be so dammed sure of yourself, Carlo. You may yet have the unique experience of losing a fight.' With that, she turned her back and made off down the iron stairs before he could come back with any reply.

She didn't know what was happening between them and she held no hope for the future, but all she could do now was go along with things and hope that by tomorrow when she had a talk with David everything would begin to make sense.

CHAPTER THREE

WHILE she had been getting changed he had booked them a table at a rather exclusive little restaurant in Hay. The car park was full of expensive cars but the cream and silver Rolls was in a class of its own. Storm felt embarrassed by its ostentation and by the contrast with the home-made dress she was wearing.

'It must look like the servants' night out,' she remarked as the soft, almost inaudible throb of the engine died away. Carlo's head turned sharply.

'What do you mean?' he demanded.

Storm picked at the threads of chiffon silk. 'One of my helpers ran this up for me on her sewing machine at home . . . If you'd told me we were coming to The Feathers I'd've rifled one of Bronwen's Diors.'

He tilted her chin towards him and looked quizzically down into her eyes. 'Why are you doing it?'

'What?'

'Putting yourself down. You look infinitely desirable, as you well know.'

Already aware that her feelings towards this man were changing drastically, she was even more confused by the new element in his own voice—the kind of seductive huskiness of a man setting out to captivate a woman he desires. Was this part of his plan to 'possess' her? she wondered.

As if reading her mind and regretting its import Carlo let his hand drop and reached almost roughly across to unfasten her seat-belt. 'You were joking, of course, about the Diors?' He raised an eyebrow.

'She's got hundreds.'

He grinned confidently. 'Not your style, anyway.

Come on.' He led the way across the forecourt into the restaurant and the maître d' swooped forward at once and led them deferentially to a table for two in an intimate corner by a window. Although the place was crowded, it gave an impression of privacy because of the discreet arrangement of the tables, and Storm was impressed by the number of stars she knew the place had been awarded. Needless to say she had never been here before, though David had once jokingly said that as soon as there was a special enough occasion he would like to book a table for them both. She looked across at the handsome man now sitting opposite her and wondered if he was aware that the head of every female in the room had turned as he walked by. At least the presence of other diners would discourage the kind of scene that had occurred in private earlier. Determined to keep things as impersonal as possible she asked, 'How did you know about The Feathers? I thought you'd driven straight up from Heathrow.'

'I employ an assistant to smooth the way for me. It's essential to eat well when one is on the move, don't you think?' His eyes gleamed in their blue depths as if something amused him.

'She must be very efficient to organise something like this from Brazil,' Storm observed in the same conversational tones.

'All my staff are efficient.' Looking at him she couldn't doubt that they would have to be, but she held her tongue, and he went on, 'Who said anything about Brazil, though?'

Her confused expression made him draw his lips back in a flash of white teeth.

'Griff lived in Brazil so I assumed you did too,' she came back.

'Oh, I do, but I'm not rooted to the spot.'

'No, I don't suppose you are!' she said bitingly before she could stop herself.

'And what does that mean?' he asked mildly.

'Well, Carlo, I suppose it means "like father like son." Griff travelled a lot, didn't he?' she replied lightly. She knew he guessed she had been about to make a jibe against Griff's philandering but something about the sudden steel that showed in his eyes, and the abrupt compression of his firm, sensual lips, sent a flicker of apprehension up and down her spine. He looked tamed and civilised sitting across the table from her now, in his dark dinner jacket and impeccable white shirt, but the memory of his savage passion as he had threatened vengeance ran like a continuous film in her head and she was frightened to do anything to give him further excuse for retribution later on.

'He travelled a lot in his earlier years, before settling in South America. He rarely left the house during the last five years, though,' he told her levelly, watching her through narrowed blue eyes.

Storm sensed that they were skimming over treacherously thin ice—earlier mention of his father had provoked Carlo to an ungovernable rage—but he himself pursued the matter, adding, 'He was a strange, eccentric man. Even his best friend would say that. Literature was his whole life. He took no interest in the family business, which was strange, seeing that he'd gone to the trouble of marrying into it. Mother,' his eyes darkened a fraction, 'well, she managed all that. She had to, there being no one else.' He gave a rueful smile. 'As a child I could far more easily imagine him as a wandering scholar than as the chief of a business empire. Of course,' he went on with a sardonic twist to his lips, 'that was when I was a child—at that time I didn't know what a man's needs can be like. I believed him when he used to talk about honesty between men and women, in relationships.'

Storm felt shocked by the bitter expression that had come into his eyes as he was forcing himself to go over the past.

'Perhaps he was honest in his way,' she suggested tentatively. 'How can we know what passes between adults—children often misunderstand situations and——'

'You think I've misunderstood him, do you, Storm?'

She opened her violet eyes very wide. 'Carlo, I don't know. How can I? But surely it can rest now?'

For a moment she watched the deep grooves on either side of his mouth deepen in anger then, as if making a conscious effort of will, he deliberately adopted a casual pose, one arm resting lightly on the table.

'You'd have liked him, Storm, just as Bronwen did,' he told her, not bothering to conceal the note of derision in his voice. 'He once told me, "Be generous, you can afford it, if a pretty bauble brings a smile to your girlfriend's face, buy her it"—but what you wouldn't have liked was what he added.'

Storm didn't ask what that was for she knew he was going to take great delight in telling her anyway.

'He said, "But remember, those aren't the serious relationships. The real one," he always spoke of it in the singular, "the one worth walking through fire for will be different."' His mouth twisted bitterly. '"It'll be open, brutally honest and passionate, and there'll be no demands, no expectations from the woman involved because she'll be strong, one who can stand on her own two feet and wants nothing from anyone. She'll be your equal. And that's the one to go for."'

'Bronwen.' Storm's eyes glistened. 'You're describing Bronwen——' Could Griff have loved her aunt after all? There was no doubt that she was the model for Carlo's description just now. With a shock she noticed that his fingers were white to the bone as they gripped the menu, but just then a waiter came up and the powerful thread of what he was unwinding from the past was broken in the disjointed conversation that accompanied his ordering of the meal.

When at last they were alone again his eyes swept coldly over her young face and his lips tightened as if in anger as he tried to explain. 'You see, Storm, like you, I was very young when I listened to all this nonsense, and I took it all in. I even imagined the woman he was referring to was his wife, my mother. I didn't for one minute imagine that all his talk of honesty was to cover the base, central lie of his life.' His eyes darkened with remembered pain and Storm wondered if the shock of learning that his father had a mistress had made the boy Carlo had been have doubts about the love he should have been able to expect from his own father.

'Mother knew, of course. She had to live through it. Suffer it. She had to go through that hell of a marriage knowing that the man to whom she was married, who had fathered her children, was bewitched by another woman. Can you imagine, Storm,' he asked softly, 'what it must be like to be married to a man whose every waking thought is for someone else?'

'It must be horrible, yes, but then, why didn't she escape? Why did she cling on to him if she felt he'd be happier with someone else?'

'Why? Because she loved him, of course, she felt she was nothing without him. One can't simply "escape" as you put it.' He raised his blue-black head and looked straight into her eyes, 'Have you never loved anyone, Storm?'

For some reason violent colour flooded into her face and she averted her gaze with difficulty. There was a pause. He seemed about to make some comment but then apparently changed his mind and instead began to eat his previously untouched food. 'There was one other thing,' he went on after a moment or two. 'It isn't done, in the social circle from which she came, to leave one's husband—whatever the circumstances. Marriage is forever.' There was an emphatic note in his voice which told her plainly that he agreed with this.

'That seems hard, it doesn't allow for mistakes, does it?' she observed mildly.

'For better, for worse, that's the promise, isn't it? That's the standard Mother lived by—better to die than be discarded. She would have had to live in mourning for the rest of her days if they had divorced.' He stared coldly into her eyes and asked on a different note, 'Can you imagine ever being trapped in a marriage like that, Storm?'

She stifled a shudder. 'I'd escape. I would never live like that.'

'Wouldn't you?'

'Of course not!' she bit back. 'Why should I?'

'Why indeed. You're free, aren't you, Storm?'

'Yes,' she affirmed with a tilt of her chin to disguise the sudden prickle of irrational fear that made doubts swarm rapidly into her mind. The man seemed to be able to implant all kinds of ideas in her head as if he had her hypnotised. She pretended to eat but in reality tasted nothing, while a battle against becoming any further subjected to his will raged inside her like a tempest.

'Father knew what it would do to her if he abandoned her and, like a true British gentleman,' he smiled crookedly, acknowledging his own Spanish blood, 'he stayed with her for form's sake . . . no doubt he hoped to be reunited with your aunt in the love nest that was being kept for him.'

'Oh, very convenient for him!' Storm burst out, unable to contain herself. 'So what was Bronwen supposed to do all this time? Mark out the days on a calendar before he could come to her?'

His eyes narrowed.

'I know you blame her,' she went on, 'but it wasn't brilliant for Bronwen either. She was a fool for him, wasting her whole life loving one man whom she hardly ever saw. She never looked at anyone else and everything she did was in some way for him and about him. She was so beautiful, warm and generous, she should have had a good man to care for her, instead of what? Bitterness, loneliness, rejection. She must have been mad to give up so much for him.'

'You of course will be more sensible when you fall in love.' He curled his lip.

'You bet,' she replied vehemently, then stopped, gave him a scowl and added, 'but I'm never going to fall in love. I've seen what it does to people, how it spoils and ruins their lives. *I'm* not going to sacrifice *my*self the way she did.'

'Love them and leave them, Storm?'

She gave a brittle laugh. 'Why not? At least, that's the intention when I get the time.'

'Is it really?' He couldn't conceal a smile. 'You talk like a young virgin who has yet to experience the passion of physical love. It's not so easy to remain as coldly calculating as you seem to imagine. But then you're inexperienced, even though you're smouldering with the fires of awakening desire. I am right, aren't I, Storm?'

She raised her chin, a dangerous gleam in the violet eyes. 'Don't patronise me, Carlo. I've been made older than you would ever believe by what's happened.'

His eyes shone wickedly. 'A woman of experience, you say?'

'I haven't had to live these experiences. Bronwen did it for me.'

'Nobody can ever do that, little one, because everybody is different, every experience is different—you have to step into the water yourself. No one can do it for you.'

She was stung by his accurate assumption that she was still a virgin and wondered briefly if there had been something wrong with the way she responded to his kisses, but she hadn't been able to help herself, his touch had wiped all thought from her mind and her response had been entirely instinctive. His eyes had narrowed and he leaned forward across the table. 'Perhaps I'll try to help you into the water myself,' he suggested with a wolfish smile.

Remembering his earlier threat she asked sharply, 'Why? So you can watch me drown?'

'I have a suspicion you're a strong swimmer, you just need to take the plunge!' He laughed aloud at the crimson blush that flooded her face, then beckoned the wine-waiter to their table. While he was occupied her mind was in turmoil. No man had ever talked to her like this before. He seemed to be able to strip layers from her, leaving her defenceless, yet somehow it was peculiarly liberating, for he was the first man openly to acknowledge her carefully hidden sexuality, and the effect was like the opening of a door into another world. One look at his powerful all-male frame just a foot or two away from her set off red warning lights and a phrase, 'too hot to handle', that, she realised now, she had never understood before, swam into her mind. She forced herself to remember that poor Bronwen had been as trapped by love as surely as if Griff had put a spell on her, and she herself had no intention of ignoring such a singular lesson—no matter how handsome or seductive the man was. It would be the height of stupidity, she argued against herself, to allow herself to be taken in by this smooth-talking specimen. He was just a man, wasn't he? Flagrantly sexy and outrageously good-looking—objectively speaking—he was the type who would be so used to women standing in line for him that any involvement was totally off-side, even without all the threats he had so far been making. He would be able to pick and choose amongst the exotic heiresses of the social circles within which he normally moved, and she had no intention of losing her virginity to someone who, even if he was not her enemy, could only ever look on her as a toy. Besides, she admonished herself, she was crazy even to be thinking like this, for hadn't he threatened to exact payment from her in some unpleasant though unspecified way? And even if it had only been idle words—and how could she doubt that, sitting here in the luxury and comfort of the restaurant, surrounded by politely chatting guests—no woman with a shred of common sense would let him get anywhere near her. He had simply been trying to "psych her out" because she had something—Fferllys—that he thought belonged to him. But she wouldn't be psyched into anything. Tomorrow she would check up on the legal aspect, for there must surely be some loophole by which David could help her save her home and business.

All that stuff about possessing her had obviously been meant on a purely sexual level. She didn't see the point of it personally, she told herself, turning to focus on him as she realised he had stopped conferring with the wine-waiter and was asking her a question.

'I'm sorry to have to spoil the evening,' he repeated, 'by reminding you of the precariousness of your hold on Fferllys but you may as well be in on my plans for the place, as they will naturally concern you.'

'I don't see how, if you're determined to throw me out, as you said——'

'Not so fast.' He held up a hand. 'I think the situation has changed somewhat since I said that, hasn't it?'

'Has it?' Her thoughts raced and the memory of his powerful embrace burned her cheeks, making her drop her glance bashfully. That was the only way things had changed as far as she was concerned, but she needn't have worried, for he didn't appear to notice—and why should he? He looked as if he kissed women on a pretty regular basis and one more wouldn't make much difference, she chided herself.

'You're not listening, are you?'

'Not properly. I can't seem to concentrate—maybe it's the wine.'

'Maybe it is,' he agreed softly. 'Does that mean I have

to cancel the bottle of champagne I've ordered?'

'Are we celebrating or do you always drink champagne?'

'The former, I think.'

'Oh?'

'I'll leave you to discover the reason yourself.' He laughed. 'First I'll want to have a look at your accounts in the morning——'

'What?' she bristled.

Ignoring her he went on, 'And if everything seems OK I'll let you continue so long as you comply with several conditions.'

'You'll let me continue?'

'No, re-phrase it. I shall insist that you continue.' His eyes were frostily bright as he watched her face with predatory attention.

'Insist? You make it sound like a threat, and I'm not sure I like to be threatened. What if I refuse?' she countered perversely.

'I don't think you will. You strike me as a very realistic young woman, and I'm sure you realise the difficulty of relocating your business in some other area—you'd have to train a new workforce as well as waste precious months finding suitable alternative premises. In all that time orders would go unfulfilled, clients would be lost and so on. You know all this, of course, and I now see why you were so vehemently determined not to lose your hold on Fferllys in the beginning. I'm afraid I made the mistake of putting it down to sentimental attachment to the place—in addition,' he smiled narrowly, 'to an awareness of its market value, of course.'

It hit her with unpleasant suddenness that he was a far more dangerous enemy than she had given him credit for and that his earlier threat of wanting to possess her had been no idle boast. All the time she had been showing him around the studio, and even as they had been dining here this evening, his brain must have been clicking over the possible ways in which he could avenge the wrong he imagined had been done. Now he had hit on the simple expedient of taking over her livelihood. Frantically she racked her brain for a way out, but she knew it was no use arguing at this juncture.

'You mean, either I give up the business with all the ensuing hardship that would bring in its wake for everyone else, while I escape relatively unscathed—I'm young enough to be able to find work elsewhere—' she said, 'or I give in to your conditions, whatever they are, and ensure that Megan and the others don't lose their jobs?'

'It would be a poor way to repay their loyalty by ditching them when, at the risk of only a little unpleasantness yourself, you can save them,' he agreed. When he noted the sign of defeat on her face he nodded approvingly. 'I knew you'd see sense.'

I didn't say I'd made up my mind, did I?'

'Do you have a choice, Storm, when you really think about it?'

'I'd like to know more about the conditions first,' she stalled, determined not to yield all at once.

Just then, as if on cue, the waiter slid the trolley bearing a silver champagne bucket alongside their table and with a theatrical gesture grasped the bottle in both hands to de-cork it for them. As if it was a celebration and not a rout, he let the pale blonde liquid cascade festively into fragile-stemmed glasses, then with a small bow retreated as discreetly as he had arrived.

'We'll talk about conditions somewhere else,' he continued as soon as they were alone again. 'I think you've got the gist, and as your acceptance of my offer includes the whole deal the details are neither here nor there.'

'You'll never get me to do anything I don't want to do,' she told him with a spirited lift of her head.

'My dear child. I'm not a barbarian.' He laughed

deprecatingly. 'The pleasure will lie in persuading you to *want* to do what you think you *don't* want to do. And surely I've already demonstrated that I'm eminently capable of persuading you to do what I want? I would prove it again, just to settle any doubts in your mind, if I didn't know such behaviour would get us thrown out of here.' His eyes burned blue and a wave of panic surged through her entire body at the memory of the shocking ease with which he had plotted to ensnare her, playing on her weakness. It took all her courage to look him in the eye.

'So I'm to be nothing more than a captive?' she stated in a flat voice.

'If you wish to put it that way. I think you'll be a willing captive though.'

'Just like Bronwen.'

'Precisely.'

She looked wildly up at him but he had raised his glass in a sort of toast, and when she failed to comply he merely sipped his own drink and laughed softly at the panic on her face. She blinked rapidly, to force back the tears of helplessness that threatened, and noticing, but misunderstanding the reason, he snapped harshly, 'Don't try that on, sweetheart. I told you, I'm made in a different mould to my father. *I'm* the one who calls the shots, and I've already warned you not to expect to get away with anything. Somebody's going to pay and it's going to be you.'

'It seems strange,' she said, 'how your voice can switch from a hypocritically seductive caress to this cold, hard, implacable vengefulness in a single moment.'

'When somebody hits me,' was his riposte, 'I hit back.'

Storm tried to grasp at some element of the ordinary to deaden the shock waves that were still reverberating through her mind, but all she could think of was the power he would have over her once he controlled her business.

'How much control will you want?' she asked bleakly. 'Over the company, that is.'

He smiled faintly at her correction. 'Very little. You'll continue to hold the purse strings, if that's what you mean. It's entirely up to you whether you make or break yourself in the business world. I shall require a percentage of your turnover to cover your use of my property, but I don't imagine you make enough with your present means of production to pay a realistic lease. When and if the day comes that you can—I shall probably decide on a time limit—I will probably lease the studio and workshop to you at the market price. I haven't decided yet what I shall do with the rest of the place. There are certain things to be taken into consideration, don't you agree?'

Storm began to shake uncontrollably and when he lightly touched the back of her hand across the table she recoiled as if stung.

'We'll go soon.' It was said in such a way that it sounded like a threat but she forced herself to hold her fear in check so that she looked almost nonchalant as she swirled her champagne casually in the glass before draining it.

By the time they came to leave the restaurant it must have been quite late, for the car park had almost emptied and the Rolls looked sinister standing by itself under the shadow of some trees where he had parked it. It was like a nightmare vehicle waiting to carry her off up the mountainside to her fate.

Unused to alcohol, she must have drunk too much, for she stumbled and felt his arm snake swiftly round her waist as he tried to guide her across the car park. His amused glance caught her own startled look as his grip tightened, making her freeze in alarm at the contact.

'Relax, darling. I'm not going to hurt you.' An involuntary shudder ran through her to hear the suggestive menace in his laugh as he steadied her before going round the side of the car to unlock the door.

The journey back up the winding road in the darkness, with the black slopes closing in on all sides, registered only dully, and it wasn't until she realised that the car had come to a halt in the mist-wreathed courtyard that she realised she must have dozed off. An icy blast of damp mountain air brought her sharply to her senses as he opened the door to allow her to get out, then before she knew what was happening, she felt strong arms gripping her slim body, forcing a little whimper of fear from her as she was hoisted effortlessly into his arms and carried bodily across the courtyard towards the shuttered house. Somehow he must have already extracted the key from her grasp, for she heard the rasp of metal in the lock and the timbered door swung back with a sinister groan. Cursing slightly as he fumbled around for the lights, he lifted her up into his arms again then deliberately started to mount the stairs with her in the direction of the bedrooms.

In a confused blur of arms and legs she was tumbled down on to something soft and yielding and when she felt the invasion of his hands on her body she began to struggle wildly against the figure that loomed over her.

'Keep still, damn you. You'll tear your dress!' he ordered thickly.

She felt the silky chiffon slither down over her bare limbs, shivering violently as she focused on the smouldering blue eyes that burned out of the darkness and traced a slow trail over her naked body.

'Get under the covers, you're cold,' she heard him rasp as he switched on the bedside lamp. As she tremblingly obeyed she was astonished to hear him say, 'I'll be back tomorrow morning. Don't try to run out on me because I'm not in the mood to be generous. Understand?'

She nodded, too surprised that the feared retribution was not yet to come to do more. Then, before she could take in what was happening, his arms came firmly down on either side of her head; as her face tilted up and her lips parted slightly in astonishment she felt his warm lips come down firmly over hers and the gentle torture of his tongue begin to coax an instant response from her, sending subtle fires flaring through her body. When his mouth left hers the severance was like a physical pain, making her cry out his name, but the blue eyes gleamed enigmatically in the light beside the bed and before she could bring herself down to earth he had turned and left the room, closing the door behind him with a firm click.

Automatically her hand went up to finger her lips in wonder. It was earth-shattering, his touch, the feel of his body against hers, awakening some deeply slumbering core within her being. All at once she was angry with herself, for that was just the response he was hoping for and he was so sure of himself that he had already warned her what form his vengeance was going to take. He was going to possess her and he was going to make her hurt.

The memory of last night's kiss was still burning in her mind when a soft voice behind her made her pencil skid across the paper.

'I've never taken a woman when she was too drunk to know what she was missing,' Carlo murmured with embarrassing intimacy in her ear. He had come to stand behind her where she was pretending to work at her desk in the studio next morning.

'I'm telling you that just in case you're wondering why I chose not to follow through.' The glance that swept over her body stung an immediate retort from her despite her shaking hands.

'You're a great one for making choices. One of these days you'll find they've run out for you.'

His husky laugh marked his disbelief and she withstood the full blast of his ice-cold eyes on hers with the utmost difficulty.

'Did you get your account books out for me?' he

reminded, not taking his eyes off hers.

'They're in the filing cabinet over there. Get them yourself,' she replied rudely, making a show of getting on with her work.

'Got a deadline, have you?' He tapped the paper on which she was working.

'We always have deadlines.'

'That's how I prefer to work, too,' he replied enigmatically as he sauntered off.

She caught sight of him a few minutes later, clip-file in his hand, with an elderly, balding man in a dark green quilted jacket. They were walking across the yard in the direction of the house. 'That must be the surveyor,' she surmised, turning to Megan, who had just appeared at the top of the stairs and was hovering with an anxious expression on her face. 'And the other one is our new lord and master,' she supplied sarcastically. Briefly she outlined what had happened the previous evening, glossing over the details of what Carlo had called 'the deal' by merely telling her that they were probably going to be allowed to stay.

Later, during the coffee break, she knew they would all want to know more but, as she pointed out to Megan, she knew very little herself, and they would all have to wait until he decided to talk to them personally. She had rung David and he had promised to look into the possibility of any legal loophole, but her heart sank when she heard him tell her not to hold out too much hope. A sudden longing to be with him, to have that uncomplicated if rather predictable companionship he offered, made her ask him if he would like to come over to supper that evening, but he regretfully mentioned some golf club committee meeting which he had to attend and she rang off feeling more alone than before she had spoken to him. Throughout the morning she saw the two men, Carlo and the surveyor, appearing and disappearing between the crenellations on the roof. He must have found the key hanging up in the kitchen himself, she thought, and she felt even more keenly the sense of invasion into what had always been a private and protected domain.

As she expected, he eventually came across to the workshop and chatted to the women as they carried on with their work at the printing tables. Hearing his voice below, she was undecided whether or not to go down until Luce came upstairs for something.

'I'll come down with you, Luce,' Storm told the younger girl, 'I may as well hear what he has to say—he may have more surprises up his sleeve!' Her tone was light, but her heart felt like lead. When they both went back down he was laughing at something Phyllis had just said, his head thrown back and an expression of such relaxed good humour on his face that she realised she didn't really know the first thing about him. It was a shock to see how handsome he seemed even now when, after all he had said and done to her, by rights her hatred of him should have been stark and unequivocal.

Wearing tight designer jeans and a thick wool sweater in black to match the untidy shock of jet-black hair, his deeply-tanned skin gleamed with the attractive aura of a man at the peak of physical fitness. He swung his broad shoulders round as she reached the bottom of the iron stairs and for a brief, revealing instant their eyes met in an unashamedly intimate exchange.

'Fascinating stuff, this, Storm,' he told her. 'I never realised what intricate designs you can print this way. It looks so—er——'

'"Primitive" was what you just said,' remarked Phyllis with a smile.

'I'll retract that.' He turned to the older woman, then back to Storm. 'Your influences appear to be eclectic, to say the least,' he said levelly.

'Bronwen's influence was William Morris,' Storm replied, 'and that's why she always insisted we print by hand.' She launched at once into a detailed account of the different techniques they were using, in order to cover her confusion at being in such close proximity to him, with so many watching eyes—the women would be able to read her feelings for him written on her face as plain as day if she wasn't careful.

'Magic,' was his verdict as she eventually came to a halt. 'Have you ever thought of studying abroad, in, say, Japan or Indonesia?'

She shook her head. 'Bronwen has taught me everything I know——'

'I remember suggesting that last night,' he replied in the same even tone, though he laughed when he noticed the blush that stained her delicate skin. She knew exactly what he meant without having to register that bright, taunting look in his eyes. Fortunately the women were busy and, although tuning into the conversation as it took place across the workshop, weren't paying much attention to the expressions of the speakers.

Carlo took advantage of this to give her a long, lingering look that effectively stripped her of every thread of clothing, and when he came over to her he knew exactly how she felt because he said quite audibly, 'Patience, little one. It won't be long now before you start to ask.'

With a lift of her head she replied clearly, knowing that even if her words were audible to them the women wouldn't know what she meant, 'Oh, I don't think I'll ever do that, Carlo. I'm rather fond of making choices too, you know, and I can assure you that's not going to be one of them.' Her hair was loose this morning and she deliberately let it flare out as she pivoted and made for the stairs.

'Wait.' He placed a warm hand over hers as she gripped the rail. 'I need your help.'

'Oh yes?' She tried to outmatch his coolly amused stare with a detached one of her own, despite the fact that her heart had begun to pound warningly at his warm touch and at the sensation of having her hand trapped tightly though discreetly beneath his, just as she herself was being trapped by his persuasive charm.

'Yes,' he repeated. 'I brought some lunch with me from the hotel and I thought that while we're eating you can tell me a little about Fferllys—architecturally, I mean. I wouldn't want to come blazing in and desecrate the place with a lot of insensitive innovations.'

'You wouldn't?'

He gleamed wolfishly at her veiled insult. 'No, actually.'

'You do surprise me.'

'You haven't seen anything yet. I'm full of surprises.'

Her hair prickled up the back of her neck as he stroked the inside of her wrist with one finger, out of sight of the others. 'Don't do that,' she was provoked to say in a low, venomous voice.

'Why not? Don't tell me you don't like it?' he breathed softly pretending to look surprised, and she answered in a fierce whisper, 'You know I damned well don't——' at which he merely chuckled and replied huskily, 'The lady doth protest too much, methinks.' But he released her and swung briskly away in the direction of the courtyard where the surveyor, having finished his job, was already sitting in his car ready to leave.

Storm was only glad that he was at present so busy he would be hard pressed to find time to put his threats and promises into effect.

It was lunchtime before he appeared again.

'So you're fully committed to running the place with an almost total absence of machinery and with not a vestige of high tech allowed over the threshold, are you?' he began as soon as they were all seated round the big, old-fashioned refectory table in the warm kitchen where they habitually ate lunch.

'It's best this way, you see, for the effects we can get,

like,' Phyllis explained in her lovely Welsh voice. 'You can't do what we do with a lot of machinery.'

'I just love the smell of the printing inks,' came in Luce, 'and the individuality of each print—no two ever alike. That's something you can't get with machines.'

'Storm's studying batik and that's all hand-done,' remarked Megan, making Storm scowl at the look of interest on Carlo's face. There were some things she didn't want this intruder to know, and that included everything to do with her private hopes and ambitions. What he was doing now, she surmised, was trying to draw everyone out, having spent the morning going over the books with an accountant's meticulous attention to detail, and she was forced to witness afresh that he wasn't the sort of man who took just half—he was the type who wanted everything, he would plunder the lot. And what he was doing now was what he had done when he first arrived—assessing the worth of his inheritance. Resenting the feeling that he was insidiously taking over the whole show, she couldn't help a grudging admission that he had provided a royal repast with the help of the hotel's chef, but that was still nothing to what he was planning to take in return.

The women, blissfully unaware of the undercurrents of her thoughts, chatted freely to him about their work, while Storm sat silently fuming to herself.

'And what about Fferllys itself?' he asked eventually, swinging towards Storm. 'You corrected me when I called it a castle.'

'Yes, because a castle is a defensive fortification and would have been built very much earlier, probably in the reign of Edward I. A tower house is a much more modest sort of building, self-contained, self-sufficient, and primarily a residence, not built for defensive purposes——'

Something about the amused gleam in his eyes infuriated her. He seemed to be doing nothing but laugh at her today. She tossed her head angrily. 'If you're really interested you could read it up for yourself. If you can be bothered.'

'Perhaps I will.' His malicious blue eyes held hers until she forced her glance away as if to look at the clock on the kitchen wall. At half-past everyone went back to work. It was a minute or two short but she rose to her feet anyway. If she remained in his presence a moment longer she would do something she would later regret. Everybody else got up too, but as they all began to head for the door he called her back. Rather than draw attention to her hostility by being seen to ignore him deliberately, she reluctantly turned, but as soon as the door closed behind everyone else she spun on him, her eyes flashing dangerously.

'Aren't you just the conquering hero!' she derided, not giving him a chance to say what it was he had wanted her for. 'Got them all eating out of your hand, haven't you? What are you planning—to take them over, too? I suppose you get a real kick out of trampling all over us, acting the big "I am"!'

He seemed to recoil at the ferocity of her attack, but managed to remark mildly, 'They seem happy enough with the prospect of me being in charge.'

'They would be, wouldn't they?' she railed, 'because they don't know what it costs.'

'Why should they care,' he drawled, 'you're going to be the only one to pay.'

'So you never stop reminding me. It's like the sword of Damocles hanging over my head.'

'Oh, come now,' he reproved, 'I'm sure it's not going to be *all* pain.' He smiled with exaggerated charm.

She flushed and her fists clenched helplessly. 'I hate you, Carlo Llewellyn, you're a despicable bastard, and you can do what you like to me but you'll never reach the real me, never!'

'Is that so?' His face had grown slightly paler and

when he spoke his voice had thickened, the bantering note now absent. 'I guess that's what Bronwen would say often enough to my father, and maybe that's how she managed to keep a hold over him for so long. He could never let her fade from his heart because she always taunted him by keeping that little bit back.' His lip curled in derision. 'The trouble is, Storm, as I've already told you, I'm not the soft-hearted fool my father was, and I think I've got your measure already.'

With one quick movement he swept her roughly up against his hard body so that she could feel the angry pounding of his heart against her ribs, and then he began to lower his head slowly but irrevocably towards hers.

'I shall scream——' She gasped as she felt his power envelop her.

'I won't give you the chance,' he murmured as their lips touched. Then she felt the irresistible warmth of his firm mouth plundering all the softness of her own, making her senses catch fire in a confusion of unwonted desire.

'And you say you don't want me?' he mocked, slowly caressing her undulating body so that it exactly matched his own. She could feel the hard muscles beneath his clothes moulding themselves to her own shape. 'What a pity this place is swarming with people.' He gave a shuddering sigh and gradually released her from his grasp. The cold sapphire eyes probed her face. 'It won't be long. Can you wait?'

'I can wait forever,' she snapped, drawing a shuddering breath to match his own. 'You're a ruthless bully, Carlo, and just because you know how to make me feel——' she broke off then rallied, 'It doesn't mean you can take what I don't want to give.'

'I'm going to have it all, Storm, just as Bronwen took it all. You can't win.'

His hands slid away from her body and he moved back towards the door. She watched him intently as he paused in the doorway, her breath audible from the emotional strain of resisting with her mind what her body so traitorously desired. Raising one hand he murmured laconically 'See you soon, darling!' and before she could respond he had gone out, closing the door with an audible click behind him.

She assumed he was going outside to continue with his survey even though the surveyor himself had already left, but the purring of the Rolls took her rushing over to the window and she was just in time to see the pale car edge its way out beneath the archway into the road leading down to the village.

'Maybe he's taking the stuff back to the hotel,' she surmised. Everything had been packed into matching heated boxes as if for a picnic, and Megan and her daughter had washed everything and put it back into the boot of the car after lunch.

They were full of Carlo this and Carlo that when she went back into the workshop, reluctantly, because she knew she couldn't face the inevitable questions, but she had to go back or they would have thought it peculiar. Luce was talking about his car and Storm flashed her a wry look. 'Don't be dazzled,' she reprimanded lightly. 'It's probably a hire car. He's maybe got more flash than cash!'

Luce was not to be put off, 'Who needs cash when you look like him! Scrummy, mmmm!'

Megan laughed, but Phyllis looked thoughtful after Storm had spoken. 'He could certainly get a lot of ready cash if he decided to put this place on the market, especially if he's going to carry out all the renovations he's talking about. He must have a good reason for wanting to keep it. What made him change his mind, Storm? I thought you told us he was going to sell up?'

'You'll have to ask him yourself, Phyllis,' she replied more sharply than she had intended. 'His real motives are as much a mystery to me as they are to you.' Then she gave Phyllis an acute glance. 'Did he say anything specific—about the alterations, I mean?'

'He intends to add a central heating system—and not before time.' They all laughed. 'I heard him talking to the surveyor about it—with there being no gas line up here he was asking about the possibility of oil and solid fuel.'

'He'd be mad to have an oil system. Think of the tanker driver trying to get up the side of Pen-y-Llyn! No, solid fuel would be best. That's what I'd choose.'

The women discussed the matter further amongst themselves, arguing for and against what they would do in his position, and Storm left them with a thoughtful frown on her face. He hadn't actually told her that he wasn't putting the place on the market—in fact that had been his first intention, as he had let her know in no uncertain terms. But since then he had somehow managed to let her believe that he had changed his mind—that she was going to be allowed to stay, albeit at a price—in which case, how could he be planning to sell? Worried again, she settled down to work for the rest of what was left of the afternoon, resolving to ask him bluntly next time she saw him exactly what his intentions really were regarding Fferllys.

Whatever his private vendetta against her, he had an obligation to the people who worked here, and she would insist that he put them out of their uncertainty as soon as possible.

CHAPTER FOUR

To Storm's surprise Carlo didn't reappear that day and she experienced a heady sense of reprieve when, the women having gone, she was able to sit down to a solitary meal, unprovoked by the sardonic, assessing glance of those blue eyes. With a wry grimace she observed to herself that it was a little different the previous evening when she had donned her best dress and been wined and dined in a five-star restaurant. Different, she told herself, and in most respects preferable, although, alone for once, the still-painful memory of the many happy meals she and Bronwen had shared in this very kitchen brought tears of regret to her eyes. It was an unusual experience even now, after several weeks, to be entirely alone in the big house. Bronwen, fiercely independent, had steadfastly refused to employ a housekeeper.

What Carlo was doing this evening, she couldn't imagine. Everything about him was a mystery. Although she hadn't wished to let him guess how much she wanted to ask him all kinds of questions, the fact that he hadn't even volunteered a mite of information about his activities irked her. It was typical of his arrogance, she observed. Also typical was the way he had merely raised his black eyebrows with an enigmatic lift that could have meant anything when he had brought the account books back after going through them. She herself had always been put off taking a proper interest in the way the business was being run by Bronwen's laughing dismissal of what she called 'gross commercialism'.

'We're artists, my dear. Leave the money-grubbing to those who can do no better,' she was fond of saying.

While feeling that this was probably broadly right,

Storm was uneasy at the way Bronwen would term all bills 'official garbage' and consign them to a large wicker basket underneath her desk, only emptying it, in one fell swoop, when the mood took her, which wasn't often.

Of course, now that she was in charge, she fully intended to sort things out properly. It was just that so far she really hadn't been able to find the time. Now the memory of that sardonic blue-eyed look made her decide to find out what it had been about.

Sighing she pushed her plate to one side and without bothering to wash up went across the yard to the studio.

It was several hours before she came back down and went at last into the kitchen to deal with the dirty crockery. The hot water heater, one of those old ascots popular in the 1950s, was on the blink again, and while she waited for the water to heat up she pondered once more on the changing situation she now found herself in. It had taken her a while to force herself to stop listening for the Rolls coming back up the road. It was nearly eleven now. He wouldn't come at this time of night. Both fearing and wishing that he would, she wondered again what he could be doing down in the small hotel she knew he was booked into. She couldn't imagine him leaning against a bar all night in idle banter with the locals. He was too high-powered for that, too restless. Perhaps he was working, even at this late hour.

While her thoughts flitted over the possibilities they were also busy grappling with the information she had just managed to glean from the books, and with the aid of a pocket calculator she had checked the figures several times—the figure in the bank, low, with commissions done but often unpaid for, high. Gratifyingly high, she thought, with surprise. Yet some of the work had been delivered a year, in one case two years before. Surely that was extending credit too far? She had gone carefully through their list of clients and discovered who the worst culprits were and then she had gazed out of the window for a long time, planning what she would have to do. Maybe this was the reason Carlo had raised his eyebrows in that scathing manner. She supposed it must seem very slack to him. Whatever his business she had no doubt he was always paid on the nail if his attitude to her so-called debt was anything to go by.

The water began to hiss and steam so she slammed the few bits of crockery into the red plastic bowl and slopped in some washing up liquid while she considered the problems that beset her.

By the time she had tidied round she was ready for bed, and it was with a strange feeling of expectations unfulfilled that she eventually crawled between the glacial sheets. Her last thought as sleep submerged her was of firm lips coming down possessively on her own.

Next morning, having made sure everyone had enough work to keep them going until lunchtime, she had backed the rather smart red hired car out from beneath its lean-to on one side of the courtyard and, conscious of the yawning space where the Rolls had stood throughout the preceding day, had driven carefully down the mountainside in the direction of David's office.

She had half feared to meet the Rolls silently rising up the twisting road with all the concealed power of a magic carpet, but reached the junction at the bottom with an unexplained sense of disappointment and relief that she had missed him. While she allowed that it was his right to come and go as he pleased she felt a flicker of irritation that he should simply raise his hand with a casual gesture of farewell as if he was only going out for five minutes. He must have known he would be gone for much longer. Reminding herself that her thoughts were dwelling on him to the exclusion of everything else, she concentrated carefully on her driving and reached the town a few minutes later.

She was still feeling rather out of sorts when she

reached David's office and it made her guiltily return his light kiss with more warmth than she actually felt. It wasn't David's fault, after all, she remonstrated with herself, that she was in such a bad mood.

'I say, Storm, you're looking lovely today,' he greeted her, sinking back into the brown, leather-backed chair that had presumably been a fixture in the rather Dickensian offices since his grandfather's day. He looked at her brightly, his broad, pleasant face full of an innocent school-boyish appreciation of her slim form in its smart beige wool dress and jacket.

'I've come down to pick up a buyer,' she told him. 'I'm to meet him at the Station Hotel at eleven. I just thought I'd call in to see you.'

David smiled with pleasure and with a surreptitious glance in the direction of his father's office, appeared to settle back as if preparing for a comfortable chat.

She went on, 'I was rather hoping you'd have some news for me——' and when a look of slight bewilderment showed in his eyes, she added, 'On the phone yesterday you seemed to think there might be some loop-hole by which I could fight Llewellyn's claim on Fferllys.'

The worried crease between his grey eyes deepened fractionally and there was something evasive about the way he mumbled some apology, adding regretfully, 'I think it's pretty near hopeless, Storm. Griff had a perfectly legal right to bequeath the old place to his son. It's just unfortunate that you were encouraged to think of it as Bronwen's property.' He added more sympathetically, 'When does he want you to leave?'

Storm went to the window and gazed down into the busy square. 'He doesn't. At least, he *says* we can stay.'

'But that's wonderful,' she heard him exclaim. 'Then all your worries are over! I'm so pleased.'

Her face was reflected in the polished glass and if he could have seen it he would have noticed how she bit her lip before turning with a small, fixed smile. 'Yes, it's good, isn't it,' she pretended to agree.

'So it's full steam ahead? Business as usual.'

'Well,' she paused. 'There's actually nothing in writing——'

'Ah.' David, assuming his newly-acquired professional air, adopted a more serious mien and advised, 'You need to get something on paper as soon as possible, Storm. What's he going to do, get a lease drawn up for you?'

'No, he said something about a percentage until we're in a position to pay a proper lease——'

'Shrewd man.'

'Is he?'

'Did he go through the books first, perhaps?'

'No—no, why should he?' She looked bewildered. There had been enough to think about without worrying what else Carlo was up to.

'I don't know what your turnover is, Storm, but with all these top-notch buyers coming in you must be making a pretty penny—though of course it—' he bit his lip, 'it doesn't look like it to an outsider—that old car of Bronwen's for instance,' he explained. He shrugged. 'Father was wondering whether you were able to make ends meet, but I told him not to worry——'

'Carlo saw the books afterwards actually,' Storm was piqued by the fact that he and his father had obviously been discussing her affairs between themselves. She rubbed the back of a hand irritably across her brow. 'I hate all this. It's so——' She struggled for a word that would express the depths of her dislike.

'I expect you feel out of your depth,' David supplied smugly. 'But trust me, Storm. I'll advise you. Just remember this, whatever his terms are, talk them over with me first, then make sure you get it in writing. I'll handle it all for you.'

Storm could barely resist a frantic giggle at the thought of talking over Carlo's 'terms' with David, and as for putting it in writing! She felt a hot blush course rapidly up her body and she swung back to the window to rest her burning forehead on the glass. Am I doing the right thing? she asked herself, feeling drained by it all. 'Oh hell!' She swung back. 'I must dash or I'll miss my client.'

'Get everything settled as soon as you can,' David rose from behind his desk, 'that'll stop you worrying.' He came round and took hold of both her hands. 'You're looking strained, take care.'

She shut her eyes as she felt his light kiss on her forehead before opening them to say, 'Thank you for being so sweet, David. I'll be in touch.'

'I certainly hope so—you haven't forgotten our date on Saturday night, have you?'

Noting the momentary look of hurt pride in his eyes she fibbed, 'No—no of course not.' She touched his cheek with one hand. 'How could I?'

Once outside she tried to concentrate on what she was going to say to the buyer when she met him but it was impossible to think about work with such conflicting thoughts pulling her first this way and then that. Waiting for the day when Carlo would decide to call in what he claimed she owed him was turning out to be a nerve-racking experience.

Nick Gorris was a partner in a new, young, rather outrageous fashion team that had made a big hit with its first collection at the recent London Fashion Week. Storm's name had been mentioned to him when he had been making enquiries about some of the fabrics one of her clients had been using, and while she had been down in London attending some of the shows with Bronwen she had met him briefly at an over-crowded cocktail party in one of the hotels where the shows were being held.

They had had one long, disjointed conversation about

collaborating on Nick's new spring collection, both of them having to shout above the hubbub of party chatter and the distraction of camera flash bulbs. But first impressions seemed to show that they were going to get along well. Storm was pleased. She wanted to find other outlets for some of her more exciting hand-printed designs, ones she had so far been producing for pleasure rather than for profit. Before Carlo came crashing into her life, working with Nick had been uppermost in her mind. He had struck her as dynamic, though rather brash, and shrewd as well as outrageously original in his ideas, but as she walked into the sombre oak-panelled foyer of the town's biggest hotel, where she had arranged to meet him, she admitted to herself that she was feeling rather nervous now about what to expect. Such was her preoccupation that she didn't notice the tall, broad-shouldered man detach himself from behind a copy of *The Times* only to sink back behind it as she passed through the lounge on her way to the breakfast room.

Nick was already waiting, his extraordinary check suit, a key feature in his menswear collection, she remembered, being totally out of place in the quiet country town where conservatism in dress reigned unchallenged. Oblivious to all this, he came towards her with outstretched hands.

'Storm, save me!' he greeted her. 'I've just had to suffer a blow by blow account of one man's battle against a giant salmon. I'd no idea I'd be so close to nature in the raw.' He fell into her arms, managing to kiss her on both cheeks before stepping back more calmly to have a proper look at her.

'Mm, the colour suits you and I like the way the material falls, but it's rather down-in-the-country for you, isn't it?'

She laughed at his single-minded attention to style. 'See it as natural camouflage,' she replied. 'Did you have good journey down?'

'I expect so. I slept most of the way to my astonishment. There's something rather decadent about travelling by sleeper. I'm only sorry I didn't stay awake to savour every last moment of it.'

'The car's outside,' she told him briskly. 'You said you had to be back in town by this evening so we can go whenever you're ready.'

He pushed his unfinished roll to one side. 'Let's go, then. Is it far?'

'As the crow flies no, but by car about twenty minutes.'

'And which mode of transport are we using, did you say?'

'Well there's no giant crow parked outside,' she laughed, joining in his whimsical mood.

'Thank the lord for that!' He put a protective arm around her waist and was just about to shepherd her through the swing doors leading back into the foyer when they almost collided with a figure coming in the opposite direction. Storm in fact felt the imposing suit-clad body graze her own with a touch like a million volts before she rocked back against the startled Nick out of harm's way. 'Carlo!' she squeaked before she could recover from the shock of literally bumping into the man of her worst fears.

The look of heavy menace he gave her changed to one of detached politeness as he shot a glance that was a blatant and calculated assessment of the man by her side before asking, 'Going so soon, Storm?'

'As you can see,' she replied coolly.

There was a pause that seemed to stretch into infinity while Carlo waited, blocking their exit, with the obvious expectation of being introduced. Storm thought, I'll be damned if I'm going to introduce him to my clients, he's got his nose too deep into my private business affairs already, and she was about to sweep by without another word when Nick stretched out his band. 'Nick Gorris,' he announced. He didn't elaborate and Storm wondered if he seriously expected the name to mean anything to Carlo who merely nodded, murmuring, 'Carlo Llewellyn', in reply.

'Oh, a native! How unexpected!' exclaimed Nick with frank surprise, staring at Carlo's exotic foreign tan and blue-black hair, and in order to forestall the beginnings of a lengthy conversation that threatened to ensue, Storm had to say, 'We'd better get a move on, Nick. Time's running out.' She side-stepped to let him follow her through the doorway as Carlo held it back for them both and as she moved past him he murmured suggestively, 'It certainly is!' Startled, it took her a few seconds to realise what he meant. Time, he was implying, time was running out for her. And last night he had told her the same thing in slightly different words.

With an urge to get as far away from his menace as possible she almost ran across the foyer, leaving Nick to trail along behind her with the tails of his overlong jacket flapping wildly behind him.

The Welsh countryside had never looked prettier as they drove the few miles up to Fferllys. Sheep were dotted across the mountain slopes like crumbs on a green cloth and Nick exclaimed with a city-dweller's delight at what Storm usually took for granted.

'I can quite see why you remain in your mountain eyrie, Storm, it's quite delightful, though I must confess I myself would probably be screaming to get out after a week.'

'As long as that!' she remarked, forcing the labouring car round the last bend in the road so that the house loomed straight ahead.

'Oh, pretty!' he exclaimed again. He alighted as soon as they pulled up and stood in the middle of the courtyard emitting cries of approval. 'It has just that air of slightly derelict charm one expects in the country,' he remarked, then laughed apologetically, 'I'm sorry. I'm not criticising. I think it's lovely.' He gazed round at the mellow grey stone crawling with early roses and at the big stone urns placed haphazardly round the courtyard that were just now brimming with narcissi.

'It's all right,' she assured him, coming round the car to usher him towards the studio. 'It's not mine anyway.'

'How wonderful to have its use, but none of the responsibility!'

She laughed unexpectedly. 'Yes. I hadn't thought of it like that.'

'Who's the unfortunate person responsible?'

She grimaced. 'The man we've just *met,* if that's the word.'

'What? Our brief encounter at the hotel?'

Storm nodded.

Nick gave her a sudden narrow-eyed look before commenting blandly, 'No doubt he thinks it worth his while—personally I'd sell it and realise a bit of capital.' He gave a laugh. 'But perhaps he's stinging you for rent, is he?'

'We're hammering out a mutually acceptable agreement,' she told him more airily than she felt. Holding the door for him she added hurriedly, 'Go up the stairs. I'll just let Megan know we're here.'

While Nick negotiated the narrow spiral stairs into the studio, Storm popped her head round the door to see if everything was proceeding smoothly. Already the drying racks were filling up with lengths of fresh print, which hung like multi-coloured banners down one side of the rectangular room.

By two o'clock they had cleared the main part of their meeting and having already had a light working lunch had come to a general agreement over designs, fabrics and delivery deadlines. Now they had retired to the more comfortable surroundings of the first floor sitting-room to have a well-earned drink.

This was part of the discussion that Storm felt least confident about as it would concern negotiations over prices and commissioning fees for the exclusive rights to the designs she was going to do. It bothered her somewhat to feel that however successful one of her designs might be she would never be able to offer it to another client, but this was one of Nick's most stringent demands. 'I'm not into chain-store fashion,' he told her on their first meeting, 'and I don't want to see the same dress fabric turning up elsewhere.'

That had seemed reasonable to Storm but the best method of pricing something so exclusive was difficult to judge without the advice of someone more experienced than she was in the marketing side of the business.

She was just on the point of handing Nick a whisky and soda and puzzling over what she was going to say when the door burst open without warning and Carlo stalked in looking as lethal as a jungle cat.

'I'm just in the middle of a private discussion with Nick——' she began in a tone that must have clearly come over as a reprimand to him for barging into what were still her private rooms, when he replied smoothly, 'Oh good. I thought I was going to be too late. My meeting with the architects took rather longer than expected.'

He spoke in such a way as to suggest that she was party to all his plans, and as if to compound this impression he strode over to her and gave her a light kiss on the side of the neck. 'Right. Give me a run down on the state of play so far.'

He smiled with what could only have been a thin veneer of genial charm at Nick, then looked enquiringly at Storm.

'I'm sorry, Carlo——' she began, then she was distracted by the apparent effect of Carlo's words on Nick, for he suddenly started to give all the signs of a man in a hurry. Knocking back his drink he looked pointedly at his watch then got up and began to gather together all his notebooks and rough sketches, saying at the same time, 'Well, of course, I don't handle the money side of things, y'know, that's for my partner.'

He gave Carlo a swift glance. 'We were only going to try to agree the parameters of a possible price range—nothing binding at this stage. It's been an exploratory meeting, an extending of hands in greeting, as it were.' He gave an elaborate smile in Storm's direction and went over to where she was still standing open-mouthed beside the drinks cabinet. 'I've truly enjoyed our meeting, Storm. Absolutely love the designs. I'm sure we're going to be able to do business together.' He extended his hand as if to shake hers over some agreement.

Bewildered by the way the meeting was apparently being drawn to a conclusion she could only extend her fingers limply towards his. Over his shoulder she saw Carlo, a lazy smile that looked remarkably like a smile of triumph plastered across his face. If he had intended to thwart the possibility of a deal with Nick he had succeeded with devastating simplicity.

'I go crazy with anxiety about missing trains——' Nick was starting to explain.

'It's OK. I'll drive you back right now.' Damn Carlo, she was thinking, I'll talk to Nick in the car.

But Carlo rose athletically to his feet and stepped between them. 'No need for that, Storm. You've had a busy day and I have to go back to my hotel now anyway. I'll deliver Nick safely to the station.'

'Oh, but——' Her sentence remained unfinished, for as if he had swallowed Nick's excuse to get away at once he started to manoeuvre him briskly towards the door. Nick scarcely had time to say goodbye before Carlo had ushered him quickly outside.

'Well of all the cheek!' exclaimed Storm, not for the first time at something Carlo had done. She had already crossed the room before she checked herself. What could she possibly gain by going after them and causing a scene? She already knew from past experience that once Carlo had decided on something there would be no moving him. An appeal to reason was obviously out of the question. With such a man all pleas for fair play were futile.

'Damn, damn, damn,' she cursed, pacing backwards and forwards with her arms wrapped tight around her chest as she heard his car speed smoothly away. Why try to scotch a deal when it had been so near to completion? What could he hope to gain by it? Was he trying to put her out of business or what? A spasm of anger jerked through her. If that was his game he was in for a shock. It was time she started to fight back.

With a sudden cry as an idea struck her she hurried over to the phone, riffling amongst the pile of notes and sketches she had brought in with her from the studio just now, the results of her discussion with Nick that afternoon.

He had given her a card with the name and address of his work rooms off Oxford Street on it and with a tight smile she quickly dialled the eight-figure number, left her message, and with a feeling of relief that she had at least found a way to prevent Carlo getting things *all* his own way, went upstairs to change out of the beige suit into jeans and sweater. The afternoon was almost over but she had to see how the printing was getting on without her.

She didn't know when Carlo would deign to honour her with his presence again, and, she told herself grimly, never would be too soon as far as she was concerned, but she had to make up her mind to stop listening out for his car in the courtyard and get down to some serious work. When he did care to show up she would let him know that 'Storm' was more than simply a name.

It was less than an hour later when a prickle of fear ran

down her spine as she raised her head at the now familiar sound of his car in the yard. Dashing her pencil down on to the table she ran lightly to the window to make sure.

As on that first occasion she had seen him—scarcely three days ago—she was just in time to catch sight of his lithe frame uncoiling from within the confines of the car. With an athlete's loose-limbed power he loped across the cobblestones towards the house. She watched with a bitter smile as he pushed his way inside.

'Right, Mr Carlo Llewellyn, now you're going to get it,' she said aloud. Despite her brave words her heart was pounding as she sped down the outside stairs, avoiding the work room in case a word with Megan and the others managed to dilute her righteous anger. She wanted to give it to him neat.

As she flew into the lobby he was just coming back down the stairs, having obviously expected to find her in the sitting-room where he had left her.

'OK, you!' she began aggressively, skidding to a halt directly in front of him. 'So what game do you think you're playing now? How dare you interfere in my business arrangements with my clients? How dare you walk in and try to take over, you arrogant, overbearing, self-opinionated monster! I'd like to kill you with my bare hands, you—you——'

Before she could stop him he had caught her up in a bear-like embrace, and despite the flailing of her arms as she was propelled against him he effortlessly pinned them to her sides with both hands. When she looked at him there was no laughter in his face, his voice holding a harsh note of contempt that made Storm falter even in the height and fever of her rage.

'Business arrangement!' he spat contemptuously. 'Can't you see when somebody's trying to rip you off? You're as innocent as a new-born babe, Storm, and you want to thank your lucky stars I was there to put him straight.'

'What?' She gaped at the handsome face glaring ferociously into her own. 'Rip me off? What are you talking about? Don't be so ridiculous,' she stuttered.

'When I saw you with that plausible little character in the hotel I knew I was going to have to step in and sort things out. You child! Now you can just take back what you've said and thank me properly for taking the trouble to drive back up here to save you——'

'*Save* me? You're the brute I need saving from!' she stormed.

'That's entirely another matter. I'm talking strictly business now. Don't you know anything about how to handle these sharks?'

'You're mad. He's a perfectly respectable dress designer,' she began.

'He's a perfectly *ambitious* dress designer,' he corrected grimly. 'I took the opportunity to talk contracts with him in the car. When he realised I was your business manager he started to talk sense. I've got you the deal you want. So stop shouting and do as I tell you.'

Storm looked at him through a sort of haze. 'First you say he's trying to rip me off, then you say you've got a deal—I don't follow. How can I have a deal with somebody who's trying to rip me off?'

'If you only did business with people who weren't trying to get something for nothing you wouldn't do business. That's lesson one. Second lesson, make sure you get what *you* want—and that means putting a proper value on your services. If they don't want to pay a fair price that's their look-out. If you've got something worth selling you'll always find a market.'

Storm simply nodded weakly. Despite his businesslike tones she was becoming vibrantly aware of the masculinity of him, the subtle male scent of his skin so close to hers.

'Don't look at me with those dreamy violet eyes,' he intoned huskily. 'I'm not one of your damned customers.'

His lips hovered just above her own. 'You're producing some lovely designs, Storm. They're beautiful and original, but you need somebody to look after you properly.' His voice deepened. 'God, you're lovely—I can't keep my hands off you——'

His lips pressured hotly against the side of her neck as his hands began to mould her pliant body to the contours of his own; although it crossed her mind that she was supposed to be angry with him and that this wasn't exactly the way to show it, she could only return his kisses in a fever of sudden arousal that shook her with a sexual force she had never felt before. Again and again his mouth ravaged the sweet honey of her own as her lips parted in a totality of giving that had no restraint. He groaned as her body undulated against him in a fever of desire as she surrendered to the yearning to experience everything he had to give.

A sound outside the door penetrated dully into her consciousness but it was Carlo, the more experienced, who managed to bring them to their senses, pushing her feverishly away as the door began to swing open.

It was Phyllis. For a moment she eyed the two shadowy figures standing on opposite sides of the lobby.

'Sorry, Storm, were you talking? I didn't mean to come barging in.'

Storm couldn't tell how much Phyllis had seen but before she could shrug the intrusion away, Phyllis added, 'I just want to get a magazine I left in the kitchen at lunchtime.'

She crossed through into the other room and the momentary respite in the engulfing tide of love-making gave Storm a chance to look more collectedly at what had been happening. It didn't make sense. How could she continue to capitulate so easily when she hated the man? And she knew, didn't she, that he was using every method in the book to hurt her as much as he believed

Bronwen had hurt Griff? Yet his touch—she shuddered—his touch was magic to her soul.

He was standing motionless against the white-painted wall with the look of a man who has suffered a terrible shock. His eyes seemed darker than the darkest pool she had ever seen and there was a tension in his clearly-defined jaw that was visible even from where she stood. Surely that wasn't the look of a man who is setting out to seduce someone in cold blood?

Phyllis came out again before either of them spoke.

'Good night then, love. See you in the morning. Good night, Mr Llewellyn.'

'Good night, Phyllis.' Carlo's voice was gruff and Storm could only croak her goodbyes.

When the door closed behind her Carlo turned on Storm with frightening speed. 'Get out of my way, Storm!'

'But——' To her astonishment he seemed to change before her eyes from the warm, sensuous man who only minutes ago had been able to light such fires of promised ecstasy inside her to the hard, cold, hate-filled man of vengeance he had seemed on their first encounter.

She shivered as the fingers of his right hand bit into her jaw bone, 'I told you to wait for it, didn't I? But you will try to force the pace!' His lips curled back in a hard smile that failed to reach his eyes. 'Tell me something before I go, Storm—would you have invited our friend Nick Gorris to stay the night if I hadn't whisked him out of harm's way? Was that why he was so keen to leave when I appeared, and is that why you were so angry with me?'

Her sharp intake of breath made him tighten his grip on her jaw. 'Oh, sorry, I forgot. You're supposed to be playing the outraged virgin, aren't you? What a pity your sexy little body gives you away so readily. You almost took me in on that first meeting of ours. You nearly made me forget whose niece you are!'

With a sudden dipping of his head she felt his lips

come down, grinding her own so that the soft flesh was forced back painfully against her teeth. The breath was crushed from her body and when he abruptly let her go she had to draw a deep breath that shuddered up her entire frame before she could raise a cry of protest. By then he was already half-way through the door. She heard it slam shut once again, cutting off the harsh sound of his curt word of farewell, and leaving her in a silence as profound as anything she had ever experienced.

Why, she asked herself, had he changed so abruptly again? It was as if Phyllis' interruption had given him a chance for second thoughts—as if, before she came in, he had been caught out somehow into betraying real feelings for her, and that now, given time for thought, he regretted this self-betrayal. But that couldn't be true, could it? He didn't feel anything for her—he felt nothing at all except dislike because she was the niece of a woman whose memory he hated. And he had vowed revenge.

But what if—her thoughts raced on—what if he was trying to make her believe he really cared for her, but daren't show his feelings openly, so that she fell for him as hopelessly as he believed Griff had fallen for Bronwen? He had acted like a jealous man just now—a man jealous of the attentions Nick Gorris had paid her. But could he possibly be putting it on? Acting like that deliberately, so she would believe he was falling for her despite his earlier vow?

It was easy to see how, if she fell for a clever ploy like that, it would be the first step on the downward path to total capitulation.

CHAPTER FIVE

THAT night was one of the longest she had ever known. After Nick's call at ten o'clock she had simply remained where she was in the chair by the phone, too drained by the flow of her emotions to be bothered to drag herself upstairs to bed.

That Nick, obviously thinking she knew about Carlo's proposed terms for the contract, was more than happy to fit in with whatever Carlo had said should have made her happy, and he seemed as desperately eager for her to design a complete range of fabrics for his next show as she could have wished.

As Nick told her over the phone, 'He drives a hard bargain, your man, but I guess if something is worth having it's worth paying for.' And when he rang off he said, 'Lovely to have met you, Storm. Cheers till our next meeting.'

It was good. She knew she should be grateful to Carlo, yet in the torrent of emotion his kisses had unleashed she could think of nothing but how to escape from him with her pride and her heart intact. He was beginning to obsess her thoughts, first making her endure the harshness of his sudden blazing rages and the coldness of that sardonic mouth as he threatened her with retribution, then at other times making her remember only the enveloping warmth that smouldered in the depths of his sapphire eyes.

I'm becoming like Bronwen, she considered dully, as she caught herself standing at the window of the tower room with its view of the road winding up the side of the mountain. I can't be like her! I won't be! I know he doesn't really care! she taunted herself. I have to resist him. If I don't, I shall find myself throwing my life away as she did, and the thought of that is too horrible to contemplate.

But when he didn't appear the next day, nor the next, she lashed herself with the tormenting thought that, despite his inheritance and despite his vow to be revenged, he had decided it wasn't worth the effort. He must have lost interest, she thought. She even allowed the hope to enter her head that perhaps he had decided to return to South America. He must have business interests there, responsibilities, a wife and family perhaps. She tortured herself with the thought that while he knew every last thing about her, except the nature of her secret desires, she was as much in the dark about who he really was than on the first day they met. Her tormented thoughts at some times led her to imagine a wife and several bright-eyed children, at others a whole harem of exotic mistresses to whom he was longing to return.

Phyllis brought her a mug of coffee half-way through the third morning of his absence. 'Everything all right, my lamb? You've been stuck up here by yourself for far too long. Why not come down and have your coffee break with us.'

'I'm OK, really I am.'

Phyllis' sharp glance took in the unusual pallor of her face and her voice softened. 'He'll be back soon, chuck, don't you worry.'

Storm's head swung up sharply but Phylis gave a little smile. 'Don't worry. I haven't said anything to the others. I only hope you know what you're doing.' She gave her a doubtful look. 'It doesn't do any good to brood, my lamb. Come down and have a chat with the girls.'

'I'm working on these designs for Nick.' The letter accepting the terms Carlo had negotiated for her had arrived in the post only that morning. After briefly sharing the good news with everyone she had retreated to the privacy of the studio again, ostensibly to work, but in reality she was sitting motionless, lost in a fog of unremitting confusion—first longing to hear Carlo's Rolls drawing up outside, then shuddering at the thought of what would happen when next he did turn up.

Shaking herself, she asked, 'How's Dai these days, Phyllis? Is the treatment doing any good?'

Phyllis' manner changed imperceptibly. 'Not too good really, to be honest, love. But there it is. It's done now, isn't it?'

Storm's heart went out to the older woman. It seemed too cruel that her elder brother should be dying in this slow and unpleasant way as a result of his years in the South Wales coalfields. They had discussed him many times over the last year but it seemed there was no cure for him.

Sighing, Storm sipped her coffee, thinking that her own problems seemed trivial by comparison. It made her all the more determined to make the business a success so that Phyllis and everyone else would benefit. What did the emotional cost matter to her really? She would survive.

The following day was a Saturday and she remembered as soon as she woke up that she had a date with David that night. They would maybe have a drink in some country pub before dining out and then perhaps go on to the Golf Club. All day long she forced herself to keep away from the high window that overlooked the road, from Bronwen's window, but the whining of the March wind in the frame began to get on her nerves, and going over to stuff some paper in the gap she spent far too long gazing down the dull, green slopes to where the road lay like a coil of grey rope in the folds of green. The more distant mountains were rough in the valleys but their tops were smooth and looked as if they had been ironed out, curving like the contours of the body. The thought led inevitably to a memory of her last encounter with Carlo and she lashed herself for letting him crowd her every thought.

It was with relief that she noticed the hands of the clock eventually crawl round to early evening. She bathed and dressed carefully, her delicate fingers plucking at the lace collar of her silk blouse to make it stand out, smoothing the folds of the full skirt of blue watered silk. His eyes, she thought, bluer than silk. The jarring note of David's car horn jerked her out of another lovesick reverie and sent her flying down the stairs to the yard.

David was coming across the cobblestones towards her, his good-natured face wearing a grin that was like a knife in her heart. She suddenly knew she shouldn't be here, putting her face up for a kiss of greeting, letting David think the brightness in her eye meant she cared for him, leading him on into a tangle of emotion that could never resolve itself in happiness.

If only she could fall safely in love with *him*, she chastised herself. Then she caught her breath—why had she started thinking in terms of love? It was hatred she felt for Carlo—the physical desire he could arouse with such shameful ease could have nothing to do with love.

In the car, she turned to watch as David fiddled with the radio before setting off, tuning into a music station.

'Is that suitably smoochy for a Saturday night?' he grinned.

'All right by me,' she laughed shakily, wishing he'd chosen something hard and tough and cynical to banish the spell of confusion with which Carlo had enmeshed her, but she made it an excuse to ask lightly, 'Have you ever been in love, Davey? I mean really, madly, so that you don't know how to think straight?'

He started the engine before replying and she noticed his jaw tighten. 'Once,' he admitted gruffly, 'but I was very young.' He laughed. 'It certainly won't happen like that again, I shall make sure of it.' He gave her a sidelong glance. 'She was much older than me. I'm glad it happened. But it was hell when she dropped me.' He laughed again. 'At least I eventually got back my appetite!'

'And was it—what was it like, I mean—physically, how did you feel?'

He took one hand off the steering wheel and patted her wrist. 'Wonderful. Heaven and, unfortunately, hell all rolled into one.'

'Did you hurt all over?' she asked tentatively.

His glance sharpened and he risked a proper look at her expression before turning his attention back on to the road ahead. 'Are you trying to tell me something, Storm? Have you met someone?'

Her silence was enough to make him say, 'We're old friends, you and I, aren't we?'

Nodding, she could only whisper, 'I don't know what to do. I can't seem to get him out of my mind. Just knowing him seems to have changed everything.'

Crazy, isn't it? Afterwards you realise you must have been deranged or something. Nobody's as wonderful as you imagine them to be, and if you can remember that, it won't hurt so much when things go wrong.'

She was grateful for the fact that he didn't need to be told that he wasn't the one. 'But what if he is as wonderful as that?' she asked in a small voice.

'Poor love, you have fallen hard. It certainly can't be anyone *I* know—the chaps around here are a pretty ordinary bunch, not the types to instil a rational girl like you with the madness of blind passion!' He glanced at her face. 'Cheer up. Remember, love's like the weather, it changes all the time.'

They had reached the junction at the bottom of the slope by this time and he gunned the engine as he took the car fast on to the dual carriageway that led towards the town.

All through the weekend there was no sign of Carlo, and Storm made a valiant effort, with David's help, to keep thoughts of him at bay. They rode on the Sunday afternoon, enjoying the unexpected spring-like weather, and Mrs Marshall, David's mother, insisted that Storm stay to dinner that evening.

'You shouldn't be alone at Fferllys, my dear. It's too depressing to be in such a big place by yourself. I used to worry about the pair of you when Bronwen——' she broke off. 'Still,' she continued in another tone, 'there was never any arguing with Bronwen once she got an idea into her head. I do hope you won't turn out to be so stubborn.' She looked doubtfully at Storm's piquant face with the softly flowing Titian hair framing it and sighed. 'David tells me you're trying to carry on running the business single-handed. I know it's the modern thing to do, but I still believe marriage is more fulfilling for a girl.'

Storm muttered something vague about how difficult it was to give it up when it was doing so well and Mrs Marshall let the matter drop there.

As it turned out Storm was persuaded to stay the night with the Marshalls. David had two brothers younger than himself and his parents treated Storm like the daughter they never had. It wasn't the first time she had stayed overnight and she knew that despite her earlier confession to David it wouldn't be the last.

The phone was shrilling through the house when she got back just after nine o'clock on Monday morning.

'Where the devil have you been?' rasped an easily recognisable voice at the other end as she rushed to lift the receiver.

'What's it got to do with you?' she countered, angry at being called to account. 'And anyway, who the hell is this on the line?'

'You know damned well who it is, so stop playing silly games,' he growled.

'Oh it must be Mr Llewellyn!' she exclaimed in mock recognition. 'I sure as hell don't know anybody else who would be so damned rude, not to say arrogant, when he phones.'

'I've been trying to ring you since Saturday evening,' he stated, as if that did away with any further need for apologies.

'So what?' she retorted. 'It's no reason to bawl at me when you do get through. Now, I'm very busy so can you please get to the point.'

'Oh, she's busy, is she?' he mocked. 'So sorry to take up your precious time, ma'am. I'm going to be making further inroads on it over the next few weeks, so you may as well be warned.'

'I understood I had already been warned. Don't you feel you're becoming rather repetitive?'

There was a slight pause and when he spoke again it was on a different, crisper note. 'There'll be builders, plumbers, electricians and eventually decorators starting work soon. They'll be working in the new wing to begin with and then they'll start on the old bit you've been living in. I've put one of my architects in charge so you don't have to be bothered with any damn fool decisions. All you have to do is to make sure thay have access when and where they want it. I'm having a full set of keys made so I'll have to borrow yours today to get copies made. I don't suppose you have a complete set of spares, do you?'

'No——'

'I thought you wouldn't. I'll be up in half an hour to get them. Be there.'

With that he rang off.

Storm was left holding the receiver, listening to the sound as it disconnected, and speechless at his effrontery.

'Don't you *dare* assume I'm just here hanging around at your beck and call again!' she hissed as the Rolls came to a stop and the door half opened. She had sped across as soon as she saw it. 'And don't bother getting out! Here are the damned keys and I want them back before five. Understood?' She was purposely keeping her voice low because the women were already at work in the print-room and its door was standing wide open. It gave her words an extra vehemence that brought a wash of pale rage across his deeply-tanned features, and his eyes began to glitter with suppressed feeling.

The violence with which he swung the car door open almost knocked her off her feet as she stumbled to get out of the way. He uncoiled to his full height and towered over her before saying through half-closed lips, 'You seem to forget I call the shots around here. Get inside!'

Blood began to pound through her veins with febrile intensity and she couldn't help taking a short step back, bringing her arms up around her breasts as if protecting her body from his touch. With a lazy, confident gesture he stretched out a hand and pulled her towards him. 'I said, get into the house. I want to talk.'

He began to half drag her towards the door.

'I'll come. Just get your filthy hands off me,' she whispered, casting embarrassed glances towards the print-room.

'Think I'd trust you further than I could throw you?' he mocked. 'I wasn't born yesterday.' Without releasing the painful bite of his fingers on her forearm he half-dragged her inside the house, closing the door emphatically behind them. Storm's knees felt as weak as cotton as a sense of privacy made itself felt. But he released her as soon as the door clicked shut and, swinging the bunch of keys in one hand, glowered at her from the far side of the lobby before rasping, 'Where were you on Saturday night?'

'Mind your own bloody business!'

'It is my business. You're on my property. I need to know what's going on. You could have been murdered by some passing motorist for all anyone knew.'

'Well, you were obviously worried about that. I suppose you called the police out?' she asked sarcastically.

'No. I took the precaution of checking up first.'

'You came up here?'

Ignoring her question he asked one of his own. 'Were you out with someone?' His voice had changed.

'Yes, with my boyfriend if you must know.'

'Where did he take you?' he asked conversationally.

'What on earth's it got to do with you?' Then she smiled craftily. 'Though if you must know I went back to his place.' She didn't add that had been on Sunday afternoon with the added presence of his entire family.

'A serious affair, is it?' he mocked, insultingly unmoved by her disclosure.

'Very,' she clipped back.

'So that might mean you'll be marrying soon and I'll be able to have this place to myself after all?'

Her jaw sagged, then she recovered and told him with a lift of her chin, 'I thought you called it a serious *affair*? I would have thought that excluded marriage. I've already told you, after witnessing what love did to Bronwen's life my motto is love them and leave them.'

'You bitch!' He gripped her by the back of the head and dragged her powerfully against his body. 'If you're ever going to live long enough to have an affair of any sort, it's going to be with me.'

'Stop it, you're hurting!' She kicked out as hard as she could at his hateful shins, but he was too quick and her foot met thin air, over-balancing her so that he scooped her up effortlessly in both arms. His mouth teased a savage trail down the side of her cheek till it fastened fully on her parted lips. With dismay she felt her body respond immediately and tears of humiliation started from her eyes. She tried twisting her head from side to side but he merely increased his grip till the yearning inside her brought a sweet resilience and her limbs seemed to melt beneath his caress.

When he finally released her lips she was breathless but managed to whisper, 'Please don't, Carlo, don't. I can't stand it.'

'You're using too many words,' he murmered seductively against her cheek, 'just say please.'

'Never,' she moaned.

'I'm willing to be the first in your career of loving and leaving,' he murmured, tightening his hold on the hair of her scalp, 'or should I say one of the first?' His lips crushed savagely, hurting her tongue. 'I could take you here and now, couldn't I, Storm?' He snaked his hands down the length of her spine in a slow caress that made her expose her slender neck in an arch of desire. All his anger was doused and another expression had taken its place, causing Storm's limbs to turn to molten honey. For a moment his short, dark lashes concealed his expression from her, but then they swept up to reveal the steel-blue glitter of eyes that slid slowly over her face in such a way as to strip all rational thought from her head, his expression enigmatic as he searched her flushed features and trembling rose-pink mouth.

'Admit it, Storm. I could take you now . . . if I wanted to.' He laughed harshly and released her as if her yearning body suddenly contaminated him with its touch.

She blinked her violet eyes uncomprehendingly as he told her, 'I'll drop the keys back later this afternoon.'

With an insultingly confident gesture he reached out and lightly skimmed her body from neck to thigh before turning briskly to leave. Storm could only lean against the wall, hands flattened as if for support, as she gazed unseeingly after him. It was humiliating, the ease with which he could turn her on. It seemed as simple as if she were a mechanical doll and he was her master. These sudden changes of mood were undermining her judgment—all she could do in order to stem the sharp pain that his abrupt rejections made her suffer was to cling to the certainty of the belief that he was doing it as a deliberate ploy with the aim of trapping her just as he believed Griff had been trapped by Bronwen. But she would fight him. Her fists clenched. She would not fall under the spell of his blatant, manipulative charm. She would force herself to see it for the sham it was.

'Oh, he's brought a visitor!' called Luce as she glanced casually out of the window later that afternoon to see whose car had come throttling in through the arch. Storm was helping in the print-room. Anything, anything, she thought feverishly, to take her mind off the storm of desire he had raised.

The sound of the door opening and the sudden hush as the women raised their heads told her that he had come into the room. Pretending to be concentrating on what she was doing, she kept her eyes down so that all she saw was the bunch of keys as a hand dropped them down on the print table beside her.

'Thanks,' came the throaty voice. 'Don't let me interrupt if you're busy. I'll introduce you to Isabella some other time. I'm just going to show her the house.'

With heroic self-restraint she didn't even raise her head as they left the room. A trail of expensive perfume was all the evidence she had of his companion's presence.

'Who was she?' exclaimed Luce in awestruck tones. 'Is it his girl friend, do you think?'

'He's not married, is he, Storm?'

'How should I know?' she replied shortly.

'I thought he might have mentioned, like,' Luce went on.

'We have a business relationship. The question doesn't arise whether he's married or not,' she repeated with an uncharacteristic snap in her voice. She felt, rather than saw, Luce exchange a look with Gwyneth.

'If I was in your position I'd sure like to know whether he was free or not——' drawled the younger girl humorously.

'Get on, Luce,' reproved Megan, not above playing the mother in public when necessary.

'Sorry, Mums, am I shocking you?' replied the irrepressible teenager.

'I'll shock you if I let on to Hughie what you've been saying,' replied her mother, unperturbed.

'She looks foreign,' Gwyneth remarked. 'All that jet black hair and gold bracelets. Very hot-blooded, the South Americans, they say.'

'There are plenty of hot-blooded Welshmen around if you know where to look,' broke in Phyllis with a grin.

'Oh come on, Phyl, tell us about him,' teased Luce.

'Isn't she the dark horse, then,' Gwyneth joined in.

Storm went to the printing schedule and pretended to check through it while the women joked and bantered as they worked. She felt she ought to be ashamed of herself for being so miserable but if she stayed here much longer amidst all this idle chatter she wouldn't be able to stop herself from screaming out loud. Forcing herself to appear under control she escaped up to her studio and when she dared she moved casually over to the window that looked over the courtyard.

It was only a moment before two figures, one painfully familiar, the other a dark and attractive stranger in a scarlet jumpsuit, came walking slowly back round a corner of the house. Keeping out of sight she watched as they stood in the yard for a few minutes while Carlo explained something and his companion, a vivacious woman in her late twenties, with gleaming black hair scraped elegantly back to reveal the jutting cheekbones of her Spanish ancestry, appeared to ply him with eager questions.

What were they discussing? wondered Storm. And

why had he brought her here to show her the house?

Laughing intimately, they eventually moved towards the car and Storm saw Carlo's arm slide protectively around the woman's waist as he helped her inside.

Did he take her to bed? she wondered bitterly, speared by the shafts of a sudden jealousy that caused her mind to spin out of control as it searched for an avenue of escape from such a horrible thought. She had never felt like this before, never, and she hated the intensity of the emotion with its capacity for destruction.

Does it matter what he does? she asked herself savagely. He's nothing to me. Damn him, damn him.

It was two weeks before Storm saw either of them again. In that time, true to his word, first an architect and his assistant, then a team of workmen moved into the place to 'tear it down and put it together again' as Raimondo, the architect in charge, remarked to her when they first met. From him Storm gleaned the information that Carlo was the head of an international building conglomerate, responsible for major reconstruction in practically every continent the world over. 'His family firm built the capital of our country,' he told her, 'and now Carlo spearheads our advance into the West.' She learned that Carlo's main sphere of operations was development in Africa, and Raimondo seemed to think that this was a reasonable excuse for Carlo to find himself in Wales.

'The world certainly is his oyster,' Storm remarked drily.

'Oysters? We eat oysters?'

Storm laughed. 'That would be nice, but it wasn't quite what I meant.'

'Yes, come, we go to Paris. I know a very nice oyster bar in the Rue St Germain. What are you doing this weekend? You're a very hard-working lady. You must take time to enjoy yourself.'

Not believing a word he said, Storm joined in the joke.

'You're quite right, Rai. I am very hard-working. I certainly deserve a weekend in Paris!'

He patted her arm, his bright Latin eyes sparkling like cut stones. Just then, the Rolls swung in through the archway and Raimondo went over to greet his boss, leaving Storm to retreat to the safety of the house. It was two hours before she heard the tread on the stone stairs that warned her of someone's approach.

It was late afternoon. Sunlight lay in pale blonde bars across the carpet, dust motes dancing haphazardly in the unusual warmth of late spring, the tender sound of young lambs bleating from the nearest hill floating in clearly through the half-open windows. A small vase of violets and snowdrops stood on the table beside her chair and she raised her dark lashes at the sound of the door opening into the room.

'What's the matter? Why aren't you working?' he demanded, coming inside and closing the door without a proper greeting. 'Are you ill?'

Storm raised her violet eyes to meet his harder blue ones.

'I'm not ill.'

'Then why are you lying on that sofa with a rug over your knees? What's the matter?'

She glanced at him with an impatient frown. 'I don't feel well. Don't they teach you anything about human biology in South America?'

'I went to school in England if it's of any interest.' He came to sit on the edge of the sofa but had the grace to look slightly abashed at his own tactlessness. 'Has anybody brought you a drink?' he demanded, looking round the room for signs of one.

'No. They're all busy. Besides, I'm quite capable of getting myself a drink. I'm not totally incapacitated, you know.'

'No, I don't suppose you are.' He eyed her levelly.

'What if I offered to make you a cup of coffee? What then?'

'I should probably fall through the floor.'

His expression was carefully guarded, assessing her mood.

'You're different,' he judged. 'It's been two weeks and you're different. You look different. What have you done?'

'What do you mean? What have I done to my appearance, or what have I done while you've been away?'

'Stop fencing. I want to know what's been happening.'

'Nothing's been happening. What should happen? I work, sleep, eat. Your people tear the place down and build it up again.'

'How do you like the new bathroom?'

'Very chic. It'll be lovely once the water's running.' She hadn't meant it to sound ironic, but he took it as a criticism.

'You're still impatient, then?'

'You've only been gone two weeks, give me time.'

'Only?' He gave her a veiled look and rose abruptly to his feet and went to stand by the window and appeared to be studying the view for longer than it warranted. When he turned back his eyes were lost in the shadowed sockets of his eyes.

'That's what I've missed about you.'

Shelving the disquiet she felt at the possible meaning his manner betokened, she felt her breath stilled for a moment. There was a full minute of silence. He broke it by beginning to pace restlessly about the room, picking things up and putting them down without really looking at them.

'Taking an inventory, Carlo?' she asked softly.

'You could say that, yes.' He swung towards her with a brief flash of humour in his eyes but when he came back to sit on the edge of the sofa, crushing her legs in the process, his expression was veiled again and he didn't explain his cryptic remark, asking instead, 'Get on all right with Rai?'

'Oh, yes. He's very nice,' Storm replied warmly.

'Hm.'

'And what does that mean?'

'Nothing special.'

Feeling that they were still fencing with each other, yet wishing to avoid the almost inevitably personal nature of anything she would wish to ask him, she said lightly, 'Is Isabella with you?' and then wished she hadn't when he replied, 'She's at the hotel.' He paused. 'They've got on well with the new wing. There wasn't so much to be done after all. We'll be able to move in at the end of the week.'

Storm felt a seismic shock disturb her—she couldn't speak for a minute. He took her silence as an opportunity to add, 'I suppose Rai must have told you how useful this place will be as the centre of communications for our European interests?'

'He didn't.'

'He didn't?'

'He didn't,' she replied automatically as if taking part in a radio game, her thoughts still blurred by the fact that he was moving into Fferllys with Isabella.

'Well that's what's happening. My role has changed recently—still, you don't want to know all that.'

Storm felt an insatiable need to know everything but she couldn't tell him that without cracking the façade of reserve she was striving to maintain. Something of her manner must have got through to him, though, for he suddenly rose to his feet with a muffled curse adding, 'You're so cold. Like an ice maiden. What is it? Some new seduction technique?'

'I leave technique to you, Carlo,' she was stung to reply. Obviously he was angry because she would not submit to his overtures, she told herself, flinching when his eyes fastened on her face. He gave her a long, hard stare that sent the blood pounding through her veins, then with a rapid pushing of a hand through his sleek blue-black hair, making it touchingly untidy so that for a moment he looked like a small boy before the purely male grace and power of him changed the image, he began to head for the door. His departure left an icy blast behind that had Storm's senses reeling as much out of control now as during his previous urgent physical assault on her body had done.

Yet, in some subtle, unspoken way she felt that she had proved a point. She had proved to her own satisfaction that she could freeze the vibrant ache of desire that his presence evoked, till it hardly hurt at all.

CHAPTER SIX

CARLO'S return to Fferllys had an effect similar to a tornado on the place and everyone was swept up in the whirl of activity in which he was the dynamic force. The entrance to the first floor gallery had already been unbricked and the dozen rooms beyond it were being made habitable—Carlo's suite of offices took precedence. His people moved in to rip out the old, highly dangerous electrical system, to install radiators, to fit bathrooms, to plaster, paint and generally refurbish the long-neglected rooms. In addition Carlo had plans for the part of the house that Bronwen and Storm had muddled along in, and she had seen him eyeing up the old-fashioned kitchen in which the staff ate lunch with a calculated look that spelled change at all cost. Not that it wasn't long overdue—it was just that, as she explained to Megan, it was a dear old place and she was fond of it as it was, blemishes and all. Megan was too impressed by the sauna which had just been installed in one of the cellar rooms to have much sympathy. 'It's a question of taking the rough with the smooth, love,' she commented.

Storm avoided Carlo as much as possible. It was easy enough. Both of them were hard at work all day, and each evening he would return to the hotel—and presumably to Isabella. Only Raimondo and his assistant had moved into Fferllys and they seemed to relish the fact that work was still going on around them. To have to live in an undecorated, half-finished suite at Fferllys wouldn't be good enough for Isabella, thought Storm secretly.

One morning Carlo did after all seek her out deliberately. He wanted to ask her what she thought of the outline plans for the new kitchen. He spread out the architect's blue-print on a table in the studio and was about to unfold the first of a pile of coloured brochures when she lifted her head from her work to say cuttingly, 'Don't ask me what I think—I have no preference either way and I hardly feel that my wishes are relevant, do you?'

His blue eyes narrowed dangerously. 'You live here. You use the kitchen all the time. You're going to be the one who's going to have to cook on a portable stove for a few days when they rip out the old cooker. I'd've thought it concerned you very much indeed.'

'You seem to forget I'm just a prisoner here. What rights have I?'

'None,' he agreed easily, adding, 'Only what I bestow on you of course. But now I'm inviting you to comment.'

Her lip curled in derision, 'I'm sure you can guess my comments without being told.'

His expression was bleak. 'Can I?' he iced back.

'Surely,' she breathed, veiling her violet eyes as she looked up at him.

'I was right. You have changed.'

'I?' She lifted one shoulder.

He rose slowly to his feet with a look of cold hostility masking his face and, forgetting the pile of plans, came round the edge of the table to where she sat until he was standing directly behind her chair. Without touching her he was able to make her body respond like a flame to the male power that he seemed to exude through every pore. 'Storm,' he rasped with quiet menace, 'do you think you can win by resorting to passive resistance?'

She daren't turn her head to look up at him because the thought of that concentrated will focused so stubbornly on her made her momentarily lose her belief that she could withstand him. 'I don't know what you mean.' she muttered thickly, bending her head as if still concentrating on the half-finished drawing in front of her.

'But I think you do,' he breathed silkily just behind her

ear. 'Ever since I've been back you've avoided me, and when our paths have accidentally crossed you've deliberately blanked me out as if I don't exist.' His voice dropped. 'You meant me to notice—your message was as unmistakable as if you'd surrounded yourself with "keep off" signs.'

'I don't know what you mean,' she repeated doggedly.

'Don't fib to me, Storm,' he mocked, 'and don't underestimate me. Remember, I still call the shots.'

Her hands began to tremble and she hunched lower over the drawing board so that he wouldn't notice what effect he was having, but he came round the side of her chair and one hand snaked out to take the pencil from between her fingers while the other lifted back the fall of straight glossy hair that swept her cheek so that her taut face was revealed to his gaze.

He laughed softly at her confusion and she bit her bottom lip to stop its trembling.

'Are you seriously hoping that by freezing me out I'm going to forget the debt you have to settle? I told you I intended to collect, and I meant it.' He touched the side of her face, following the curve of her cheekbone with the softly pressuring contact of his knuckles, insisting that she give some response, and mockingly amused when she deliberately kept her eyes cast downwards. Anything, she thought, rather than open to the thrust of those maddening blue eyes. But the tension of resisting him was unbearable.

'Leave me alone, Carlo. I don't want to have anything to do with you,' she muttered in a tightly controlled voice.

'But you accepted my terms when you agreed to stay on. You know what I require of you.'

'I didn't think you could possibly mean it,' she managed to stammer, her lips scarcely able to move.

'Do I look as if I'm joking?' he countered, tipping her face up to his so that she was forced to submit to the blaze of his eyes as they raked her expression for signs of rebellion. 'By asking me to let you stay on you consented to let me choose for you whatever role I required. In the circumstances I decided it would be neat justice if you fulfilled the role for which your aunt set the pattern—mistress of Fferllys. We are both inheritors, Storm,' he went on. 'We are linked by our inheritance. Call it destiny if it makes it easier to accept.'

His grip tightened momentarily and she stiffened as his long fingers bit into her chin.

'This passive resistance just isn't playing the game now, is it? It's a coward's way of reneging on our bargain.'

Speechless with the turmoil of emotion his touch automatically aroused within her, yet determined not to show by the flicker of an eyelash how powerfully he aroused her, she half-closed her eyelids, the long, dark lashes veiling the beginnings of desire that she knew would be revealed in their violet depths, and she was just in time to hear his sharp intake of breath before there was the sudden, sawing bell of the telephone at elbow level.

'Don't answer it,' he murmered, lowering his head until she could feel the warmth from his skin against her own.

'I must,' she managed to stammer.

Without releasing her he reached out one hand and picked up the receiver himself. 'Yes?' From far away came a man's voice. 'She's not available. I'll take a message.'

She tried to open her mouth but his grip increased. The voice spoke again. Carlo made some curt acknowledgement, then dropped the receiver back into its rest. 'David,' he told her, sliding his hand down the side of her neck, 'he'll call back.'

He raised one eyebrow as if to ask who David was and she started to say, 'Mind your own——' but before she had time to continue his lips were muffling her words and she felt her body respond as his other hand massaged the length of her spine, making the tension of resistance flow out so rapidly that she felt she had been lowered abruptly into a pool of liquid heat. Automatically her lips parted and her head arched back so that his sensual tongue could reach the most vulnerable regions of her mouth, and she felt her own tongue circle and curl and tease his own in ways she had never imagined. One hand came up to resist, pushing feebly at the muscled shoulders, contradicting the message of her mouth, but even as it pushed ineffectually at him her fingers slid amongst the long strands of thick, dark hair, turning and twisting in a fever of conflicting desire as they first pulled him towards her then pushed desperately to free themselves, then drew him down again towards her so that the pressure of his lips mingled a sharp, heady bite of pain with the liquid heat of her pleasure.

Without knowing how he did it she felt herself drawn up into his arms so that their two bodies matched line for line in a rippling contact that made them seem one. Storm's determined bid to resist him was demolished in the heat of the long-pent desire he was so expertly unleashing from where it had always been buried deep within her.

At the same time she was trying desperately to hang on to one small nub of resistance, like a small voice crying no in the bottom of her mind. Breathing heavily like the athlete he physically resembled, Carlo raised his sleek head for a moment. 'Where can we go, Storm?' he demanded huskily. The question in its brutal practicality was enough to strengthen her token resistance, and the accompanying picture of what would be involved if she should say yes brought a shudder of self-disgust spinning into her imagination, forcing her to speak aloud the denial of what her body was so patently affirming.

'I don't want you, Carlo. Please let me go. Anyone may come in—please!' Strengthened by her conviction that she must say no at all cost, she made an effort to wriggle free. 'What will everyone think if word gets round that we behave like this? What will Isabella say when she gets to hear of it?' she stabbed out.

His response was to press his lips burningly against her left temple. 'I don't care a damn what anyone thinks.' He drew curves on her skin with his lips that sent wriggles of pleasure up and down her body. 'But thanks for reminding me of something I nearly forgot.'

He stepped back and held her at arm's length. 'I think of you every night up here alone—one of these nights I'm going to get rid of Raimondo and company and come to you.'

'But you can't, can you? Isabella would wonder where you were.' Her eyes glassed over with scorn.

'And is that why you began to hope I'd forgotten your little debt? Do you think I can't handle two women, Storm?' he murmured through scarcely parted lips. Something about his manner had changed and she flinched as his eyes swept coldly over her face. 'I can assure you that presents no problem at all.'

While her body trembled with suppressed anticipation she managed to give him a cool look in response, her heart-shaped face pale in its frame of dark hair. 'I'm not interested in your prowess as a super-stud, Carlo. That sort of macho boasting leaves me cold.'

'Liar,' he murmured, flicking his tongue in a little darting motion behind the lobe of one of her ears. 'If this is you being cold ...' He pressed his lips once more against her own then reluctantly released her with an abrupt glance at the watch on his
wrist.

'Saved by the bell, figuratively speaking,' he told her suavely. 'I have an appointment with Isabella in two minutes.'

'Appointment? That's rather a funny thing to call a date with your girl-friend——' she accused sarcastically.

'But she's coming up here on business,' he informed her smoothly. 'She's much more than just a beautiful, sensual and generous woman—she's a director on the board of one of my companies.'

He left before she had time to take in what he had told her and for a full minute she could only stare after him where he had rapidly disappeared from sight down the stairs into the yard. Every word had been calculated to function as a honed dagger aimed with deadly precision at her defenceless heart. She was sure he knew how every thrust had hit its target.

Beautiful? . . . yes, she was, no one could dispute that if vibrant, glossy, exotic beauty was admired. Sensual? . . . if he said so, presumably it was on the basis of experience. And generous? . . . Storm's stomach clenched in a spasm of jealousy at the thought of what the other woman could give when she could only cringe and cry no, though her body yearned in a frenzy of desire to say yes.

If only they had met in different circumstances without the web of the past tying them into a spider-and-fly relationship—if only, if only, she cried inwardly.

It was work that offered immediate solace. With a racking sigh she turned back to her drawing board and resolved to make a huge effort to shut out the sound of Isabella's car thrumming into the courtyard. What business she could have with Carlo she couldn't guess but the result of being told this piece of information was all he could have desired, for it brought a pain like nothing she had ever felt before. He was like a drug to which she had built up no resistance, yet this deliberate, self-inflicted withdrawal from it was a kind of hell itself.

Scarcely half an hour elapsed before she heard the outer door at the bottom of the stairs open and voices echo up the spiral inside the tower. A few seconds later the door to her studio opened and Carlo entered, followed at once by Isabella. Storm had been introduced briefly the day of her arrival, the day Carlo himself returned from his fortnight's absence, and now she found herself subjected to the other woman's interested scrutiny as she fumbled in confusion at the array of pencils on her desk as if trying to make up her mind which one to use. All her self-possession seemed to have deserted her as she felt two pairs of eyes examine her with presumably such different thoughts going on behind them.

'Have you had time to cast a glance over the plans for the kitchen, Storm?' Carlo demanded without preamble as he walked over to where he had left them on the table.

'Er, no——' she began in confusion, accidentally letting her pencil fall from trembling fingers on to the floor. She bent to retrieve it just as Carlo too reached down for it. Their hands touched underneath the table making Storm jerk back as if stung. When she looked up Isabella was standing beside the desk, a look of open interest on her face.

'Take no notice of Storm,' Carlo remarked letting the pencil drop on to her paper as he turned away. 'She's a bundle of nerves these days. It's what comes of living up here with only Rai and Paulo for company.'

'That will all soon change,' Isabella replied throatily. She gave an ambiguous smile that made Storm wonder what she was really thinking—her manner was entirely neutral and but for her enviable good looks that Carlo so obviously relished, Storm would have had no reason for the suspicion that she meant more to Carlo than any other business colleague. But it didn't seem plausible to think that Carlo would have such an attractive colleague without trying to make love to her. He had said as much himself already.

As they both bent over the plans her jealousy drove her to try to gauge the depth of their relationship by closely watching their every move. Each flirtatious glance of the liquid, dark eyes beneath the coal-black lashes fanned the embers of her jealousy, and the fact that the blue eyes in return seemed to hold a special message that excluded anyone else from participating only added to her misery. Deciding that the best course was to ignore them, Storm started to sharpen one of her pencils, but on hearing the rasp of the penknife Carlo called over to her.

'This may seem irksome, Storm, but it may be your last chance to make any radical changes. Surely you can spare a minute?' He put a hand on Isabella's shoulder. 'You have to leave soon, don't you?' Isabella nodded the head of jet-black hair, ''Fraid so.'

With ill-humoured remarks flashing secretly through her mind, Storm reluctantly sauntered over to them both, placing herself as far from Carlo as she could get. She was strongly aware of the other woman's perfume and wondered how long it had taken Carlo to capitulate to its sexy message of desire—it seemed to scream that Isabella was available—generous was how Carlo had described her, she thought bitchily.

Scarcely seeing what was in front of her, she let the other woman describe the reasons for the detailing in the plan, the positioning of the various appliances, the extent of storage space and the kinds of work-surfaces to be used. It was all a blur of dimensions and comparative proportions and most of it she allowed to go right over her head until she felt mesmerised by the jangly gold that weighed down the thin, tanned arm waving in explanatory gestures over the plans.

When Isabella finished speaking, Storm nodded dumbly. She was distantly aware that Carlo had won a point—he had got her to look at the plans after all. A quickly exchanged look confirmed that he was aware of this too and his slight air of smugness made her want to reach out and hit him, hard.

'Marco will adore the place,' remarked Isabella idly as she folded all the sheets up into neat squares and placed them for safe-keeping in a smart-looking black leather brief case which she tucked under one arm.

She made her way to the top of the stairs. 'I'll get these photocopied and make sure they get to all the right people,' she said, turning. 'See you later, *caro*!' Her smile was switched on for Carlo with dazzling effect. A casual wave of the hand bade Storm goodbye and she started off down the stairs.

'*Momento!*' Carlo rapidly covered the space between them. 'Do you know exactly where all these people are, darling?'

Storm shuddered as she saw him bend his dark head to the other dark one and she turned quickly away. She couldn't help hearing them exchange a few more scarcely audible sentences and as she shot them a quick glance she was just in time to see Carlo's lips that had so recently ravaged her own with such devastating effect, brush the other woman's in a loving gesture that was quite unlike the hard, passionate assault he had inflicted on her. Miserably she looked down at her work, hiding her face behind a curtain of hair. His kisses may have told how much he wanted her, but they didn't show that he felt any other emotion for her but blind contempt for being the niece of a woman he had learned to hate.

When Carlo returned she raised stormy eyes to him. 'Does she know about us?' she demanded angrily, not caring whether Isabella was still within earshot.

'Us? What about us?' responded Carlo blandly.

'You——!' She was just about to tell him what she thought of his double-dealing methods when the phone belled again. This time she was quicker off the mark and snatched it up before Carlo could interfere.

It was David, trying again.

'I'm sorry,' she purred into the phone in her most seductive voice, 'I was rather busy——' She could hear Carlo's stifled laughter in the background. She swung round so that she couldn't see his irritatingly amused expression. 'What is it, David?'

'Nothing important,' he told her. 'I just wondered if you felt like a drive this evening?'

'Wonderful, I'd love that!' Consciously hamming it up, she was at the same time silently asking David to forgive her. She went on, 'What time will you get up here, do you think, darling?'

Gratified by her response, he said he would be along at eight.

'I'm looking forward to seeing you,' her voice dropped intimately, 'it seems so long—bye now . . . darling!'

Carlo's eyes were fastened on her in much the same way, she observed with a shiver, that a particularly hungry cat will watch a bird. She tossed her head defiantly and made as if to turn back to her work.

To her surprise Carlo got up and started towards the outer door. When he drew level he looked down, raising one eyebrow, and said, more as a statement than as a question, 'The boyfriend, I presume.' He paused. 'I wondered when you'd begin to show your true colours—"darling",' he added scathingly. With a wolfish smile that set her heart pounding again he fortunately went out, and a few moments later she heard his car sliding in first gear across the cobblestones towards the lane.

The pattern for the next stage in the transformation of Fferllys seemed to have been set, and Carlo was like a human dynamo when he was there, but there were also frequent absences when he was abroad. Storm was made sharply aware at these times that Fferllys was a very minor part of his life and that he intended it to be a retreat as well as the communications base of his business empire. It was at the periphery of his interests—and by analogy, so was she. This was cold comfort, she felt, for if she was going to be made to pay it wasn't right that something that would be so earth-shattering for her should only be a minor incident for him.

There seemed to be a pattern of sorts now that the renovations were rapidly nearing completion, for after the day's work when the labourers had all left and Storm's printing workshop was empty, she would go out with David, whose attentiveness had noticeably increased of late, or, if he was busy, she would cook in the new, streamlined kitchen for herself and Raimondo and anyone alse who happened to be staying overnight.

It was one of those rare nights when David was at the Golf Club and she was busy preparing something in the kitchen.

'Is Paulo eating with us tonight, Rai? she asked as the small, dark-haired architect came into the kitchen.

'Not tonight. Sorry, Storm, I forgot to tell you—he's taking some young lady from the village to the cinema. I think they must be eating out first.'

'No matter.' She placed a large casserole on the kitchen table. It was pleasant to eat informally like this and she was pleased that Carlo had at least had the sense to keep the fine old table that looked as if it had been made for the kitchen. She had felt uneasy at first, to be left alone at Fferllys with Rai—he was an almost congenital flirt. But once she had made it clear that she was going to treat his compliments with the same lightness with which they were given they seemed to get along all right.

A portable television had been brought up that day along with various other pieces of equipment, and after supper Rai suggested fixing the television up in Carlo's new study where, at the moment, a couple of huge leather armchairs were the only furnishings. He spent a few moments fiddling around with the tuning, then asked her what programme she wanted to watch. Preferring getting on with a good book to sitting immobilised in front of a flickering screen, she asked him to choose, hoping that if he became thoroughly immersed in something she could eventually disappear to her own room.

He had been watching only ten minutes or so when something about her manner must have told him she wasn't interested, for he reached forward and flicked off the set with a gesture of impatience.

'OK. You rather talk or play cards?'

The latter option seemed the least taxing, given that the only obvious topic they had in common was Carlo himself. Rai produced a pack of cards from somewhere and an amicable discussion about what they both knew ensued.

Compared to Rai, and she couldn't help comparing the deputy to his boss, Carlo seemed even more attractive, for whereas Rai was short, a little overweight and playfully rather than dangerously flirtatious, Carlo was sleek, sinuous and elegant, whatever he wore, with his narrow hips, sharp cheekbones, arrogant straight nose and smouldering blue eyes—his long sensitive fingers and whiplash tongue made the sense of threat he contained within his lithe muscular frame ever-present, and this was beside the verbal threats he had uttered to her. In all he was as lethal as a jungle cat while Rai was like a cuddly domestic tabby, happier by the fireside than stalking through the forest of the night.

His words confirmed this impression when, having beaten Storm soundly at a game of rummy, he broke off for a moment to show her the heavy gold ring he wore on his third finger.

'Wedding ring,' he told her with a cat's smile of complacency. 'My wife—you'll meet her soon. One day,' he told her in his attractively fractured English.

'Have you any children, Rai?' she asked, tearing her thoughts away from Carlo for a moment.

He held up three fingers. 'One, a baby,' he pretended to rock a very small baby, 'maybe Anna leave her with her grandmother some day. She's very fond mother—

doesn't like to leave the little ones behind, but frightened to bring them all this way. I tell her, Carlo look after everything first class, but she hates to fly.'

'Well I hope she'll come out soon.'

'If Carlo marries in Europe I shall insist,' he grinned at her.

'Carlo?' Her voice rose before she could steady it. 'Marry?'

'He and Isabella have an understanding, oh, a very long time. We all place bets—this year they make it down the aisle, you say? Maybe that church in the valley? Who knows?'

Striving to keep her voice steady she said, 'But surely he'll want to get married in his own country? Why choose Wales?'

'But, my dear, this is his own country, yes? That's why he sets up his headquarters here. He has come back home. One day perhaps his mother too will tear herself from the clutches of her family and come to see her son as he is? Accept him as he really is. It was a great sorrow—his father's death.' Rai shook his head, 'Carlo's mother called him "bloody Welshman". She's a very hot-tempered lady, fine figure, big—' he held out his hands, 'strong woman, head of big, big family now, a dynasty you say? Many branches, cousins, uncles, aunts. Carlo's father, forgive me, was never its head, learned man, famous, but the reins——' He grinned and held up both fists tightly as if driving a carriage, 'Mama holds those.' He had begun to chuckle. 'A dictator, yes? What she has she keeps. Everyone live in fear of her but Carlo . . . Carlo she can do nothing with. Very much alike. Fight all the time.' He shuffled the cards again. 'Come, I beat you at rummy once more then you tell me about yourself.'

He balanced a half-smoked cheroot on the edge of the ash tray and began to flick the cards down with practised skill.

Unaware of the mine he had exploded within her

heart, Raimondo complacently kept her playing cards with him until after eleven o'clock. What he had told her about Carlo's mother was so unlike the image of a frail, neglected, helpless wife that Carlo's words had built up that she didn't know what to make of it. But what he had said about Carlo and Isabella left no room for doubt—her worst fears and suspicions had been fully justified all along.

CHAPTER SEVEN

'I TRUST Rai behaves himself when you're up here alone,' remarked Carlo in casual tones when he walked into the studio next morning. 'I gather friend David couldn't make it last night?'

Storm tossed her head and didn't bother to reply but she was in time to see Carlo's eyes rake over her form in its figure-revealing jeans and skimpy T-shirt.

'When I'm not here, somebody's got to keep an eye on you,' he added slowly and with some significance.

'So who's keeping an eye on whom?' she demanded cynically.

'You're seeing too much of David,' he went on, 'he'll start to get ideas—eventually.'

'How dare you!' she spluttered. 'And anyway, what's it to you who I see? Mind your own business.'

'It's everything to me,' he murmured. 'I thought you knew that? And if I can't keep an eye on you I have to appoint someone who will.'

'And Rai's the perfect choice!' she exclaimed in derision. Let him take that how he liked!

Carlo's face was wiped pale. He thrust out one hand and grasped her roughly by the shoulder. 'So that's my answer, is it? That's all I wanted to know.' He began to haul her in slowly towards him.

'I would have thought you'd be more likely to ask him if I'd behaved *my*self,' she scoffed, tossing her head and trying without success to prise herself free.

'Yes, I don't yet know what your taste runs to—though I'm beginning to get some idea of what you like——' His hands trailed round her waist, then began to slide provocatively down the sides of her hips, moulding her against him with sickening ease. 'You like this——' he murmured huskily against the side of her face, beginning to bring his lips down so slowly she had time to feel the quickening of her own responses, her breath held as all her senses worked together in one vibrant expectation of pleasure.

'No!' she managed to croak, leaning back against the power of the arms that encircled her. 'You can't even begin to guess what I like—just because you can dazzle me with your good looks you think that's enough, but it's nothing Carlo, nothing at all! It's just surface glitter—there's nothing but emptiness underneath it. A man with real qualities, like—like David——' she improvised.

'David?' he broke in. His eyes flashed and he was so close she could see the darker rim of blue round the bright sapphire of his eyes.

'Yes, David—he's—he's worth ten of you because he's kind and considerate and——'

'And immensely dull. I can see you'd *like* him—how could you dislike somebody so bland and harmless, but you don't feel for him what you feel for me——'

'You're right! I don't—I love him. I don't love——' she gulped, 'I don't love *you*, Carlo Llewellyn!' She gave a high strangled laugh. 'It's David who really turns me on.' She ignored his exclamation of disbelief. 'You just happen to appeal to my body, you're a—a fever, a fever that soon passes . . . It's David I really love. He's worth—he's worth ten of you!' she repeated lamely.

The look of disbelief on his face was followed at once by something like hurt. His tanned features twisted involuntarily as if the wound she had intended to inflict had flashed beneath his guard before he could stop it. But it couldn't be genuine pain, could it? she judged, stifling her own automatic response to what she saw. He was out for revenge, that was all, and his real feelings, if he had any, were not involved. The shutters seemed to have come down over his face now and she couldn't read the message in the hard glitter of his blue eyes, but his words when they were eventually ground out left her in no doubt.

'You're quite right, Storm. Who cares about love? It's a fever of the imagination. What really matters is what your body is telling mine and yours is shouting plainly enough what it really wants. When the time is right——' his eyes glittered brilliantly through slitted lids, making her tremble convulsively, 'and only when the time is right,' he breathed, 'I'm going to take you and use you and discard you and you're going to beg to be my mistress just as Bronwen pleaded with my father and brought him close to ruining my family. You're two of a kind,' he rasped.

As his lips ground down on her own she shuddered with the knowledge that in the room below them the four women were joking with each other as they worked, quite unaware of what was happening on the floor above. It could only be the restraint imposed by their nearness and the possibility that someone could come up the open stairway that stopped him from carrying out his diabolical threat there and then. At night—dear god—at night was the only thing that saved her Isabella's continuing presence?

Her violet eyes gleamed in slight triumph as she realised that no matter what he threatened she was still safe. 'What a pity you can only resort to verbal threats, dear Carlo,' she said daringly. 'With so many people around all the time it must be very frustrating for you.'

'Not as frustrating as it's going to be for you one fine day, Storm,' he laughed harshly, but she could see she had angered him. 'When Isabella and I move into Fferllys—how will you feel then, knowing I'm in the next suite?'

'Sorry for her——' she replied, catching her breath but lifting her chin at the same time with a show of defiance.

'Are you positive?' He kneaded her bare midriff where

her T-shirt had ridden up and she felt his fingers caress one of her breasts, her immediate response a complete betrayal of everything she was telling him.

'Don't think I don't know everything about you and Isabella,' she stammered, flushing as his relentless touch brought her shivering body curving against his own. 'I know how she's been holding back from marrying you for years——'

He laughed openly with his head thrown back, but she went on, 'She probably got your number as quickly as I did——'

In reply he didn't bother to argue the point with her but instead dragged her up hard against him so that she became at once aware of the heat of masculine desire as their bodies met, then he brought his head down till his lips teased next to her own.

'You're a wonderful illusionist, Storm. Anybody else would think you meant all that about not caring—and for your information Isabella doesn't "hold back" as you put it, not for any reason. On the contrary——' He stopped talking and his mouth hovered tantalisingly over hers so that she prepared for his kiss by stiffening her resistance against it, yet she felt her nerves taut with anticipation as his mouth came no nearer. It would have been a small movement for her to claim that extra fraction of an inch in order to allow their lips to meet and he seemed to be waiting, willing her to make it, but, fighting back her instinctive response, she forced herself not to move towards him—it was a battle of wills, a contest to see if he could force her by sheer presence to demonstrate how irresistibly attracted to him she was, or whether she could withstand the powerful seduction of his open desire—a desire which was rapidly draining her of all resistance, even as she stood within the magic circle of his arms.

For a moment time seemed to stop its onward surge. They were so close she could see the flecks of aquamarine, turquoise and emerald that made up the distinctive shade of blue of his eyes—they had never shone so bright and silvery, she felt as if she was beginning to drown in the glittering, treacherous depths of a sapphire pool. Testing her to the limit, he forced her to hold his glance to its painful extreme before murmuring throatily, 'Yes, that's right, we do understand each other, Storm. Whatever you try to tell me, we have no need for words, you know that as well as I do.'

Her lashes fanned down over her eyes, shutting out the piercing intensity of his scrutiny that seemed to strip her down to layers of sensitivity way below the threshold of her defences, and as if she did not know he had once again entered her soul, she replied in an attempt at flippancy, that could not quite hide from herself at least the shattering effectiveness of his charm.

'Quite a technique you've got there, Mr Llewellyn. You could always get a job as a stage hypnotist should your business consultancy fail.'

Despite her words her body gave a betraying tremor as his hands savoured the touch of her silky skin underneath her T-shirt and his fingers found a way under the soft cotton of her bra so that he could caress the bare skin with breath-stopping movements of long, sensitive fingers.

'And now we've established just how much effort it takes you to resist me——' he spoke slowly, thickly, as if with a great effort, still kneading her flesh rhythmically in his warm hands, 'perhaps you'll answer my question?'

'What question?' she asked in a haze of desire, finding herself unable to focus on anything but the mesmeric touch of his hands on her smooth skin.

'My question about Raimondo. Given that you might feel no need to resist him——' he began.

'You mean you're *jealous*, Carlo.' She stated flatly with a violent flash of insight, quickly stifled.

'Not at all,' he countered with what looked like a deliberate deadening of emotion. 'I like my employees loyal, that's all. And it's actually you, as you guessed, that I don't trust. I simply want to know what his point of resistance is.'

'You mean like putting someone under torture to find their breaking point?' she queried innocently.

'Something like that,' he agreed, a touch sardonically.

'That fits,' she observed. 'That's exactly your approach to me, isn't it?' She tried to curl her lip in derision but felt the effect was spoiled by the way she was failing so abjectly to free herself from his embrace. 'Why ask me, though, for you surely wouldn't believe anything *I* told you.'

'Not your words, no, but as I've said, you have extremely eloquent eyes.'

'Please let me go now, Carlo.' Suddenly the strain of being teased like this was making her nerves ragged. Her bottom lip began to tremble and she twisted away, trying to wriggle out of his grasp, using all her force. To her surprise he let her go. 'I hope you're going to be able to concentrate on your work this morning, Storm. Who knows, maybe I'll be able to get a little privacy for us somewhere and your words can really be put to the test?'

With a twist of his lips he turned to the desk below one of the windows. He had asked her earlier if there was room in her studio, until the contractors had finished installing the last of the equipment in his own large office across the courtyard, to work at one of her tables. For some reason she had imagined Raimondo would be using it and had said an immediate yes. Now, with a sudden sinking, she realised he intended to work at the desk himself. The thought of being cooped up in the same room with him all day was anathema to her but he was already opening his brief case, reaching for the telephone, leafing through a file with cold efficiency that suggested he had immediately forgotten her very existence.

She could only turn back to her own work, as if

following suit—as if she could do any work with him in such violently close proximity. Every time she raised her head her glance fell on the lithe, muscled frame sitting so nonchalantly across the room from her. His blue-black hair was ruffled where he repeatedly ran his hands through it, and the sleeves of his black shirt were rolled to the elbows revealing his powerful, tanned forearms with the flecks of black hair on them. If she reached out she would be able to run her fingers over the corded muscles . . . Instead of the formal business suit he was wearing black jeans as well as a wool shirt, and they hugged his muscular thighs like a second skin. Something about the easy way he was lolling in the chair, as if somehow more at home outdoors than in the confines of an office, made her imagine what his life back in South America must be like—she could easily picture him riding a half-tamed stallion, rounding up cattle like a cowboy, slouching sexily through innumerable movies where the hero always gets the girl. This time, she thought, I'll have to make sure it's a different ending.

Effortfully she made herself concentrate on the intricate design, the first in the series destined for Nick Gorris' fashion house, that was spread out on the drawing table in front of her. About an hour later she flung down her pencil and began to head for the stairs. It was impossible to work next to him like this for she was conscious of every single move he made, though the way he kept his eyes fixed on his work seemed to suggest that he was totally unconscious of her presence. Only the way his glance flicked casually across the studio every now and then hinted at any other possibility. It made her nerves stretch like steel wires under extreme tension and she knew she would only be happy when she was somewhere where she would not be taunted continually by the emphatic allure of his sex appeal.

Seriously considering whether to gather her things together and go to work in the house instead, she crossed the courtyard and went into the new kitchen to get herself a cup of coffee from the new machine.

As she looked round the kitchen, she had to give him his due, he had certainly improved things out of all recognition. The kitchen was attractively done out in white and beechwood with black glass-fronted appliances, all custom-built and installed, she realised, with the sort of speed and efficiency only vast wealth can command. She had to admit, despite herself, that all of his innovations were extrememly tasteful, in keeping with the style of the lovely old building without being heavy or difficult to run. It made keeping house, even in what was now quite a large place with the potential for housing up to a dozen people, a job that was simplicity itself.

It still wouldn't stop Carlo from bringing his full-time chef and housekeeper. He had warned Storm to make the most of the kitchen when she had involuntarily expressed her delight in it, because when the chef took up his post she would no longer be allowed to interfere in his domain.

'He's simply the world's best cook,' he told her.

'It seems rather selfish of you to keep him to yourself then,' she had criticised.

'But I shan't. That's the point. Fferllys is going to be the place where I entertain my clients.' He had given her a strange smile then. 'Should I say where *we* shall entertain my clients?'

His words came back to her now and she shuddered. She recalled what he had said when they first met, in that first threatening speech when he had told her that he was going to force her to play any role he wanted. The implication had been entirely sexual. After hoping he had changed his mind it now looked as if he was still planning on carrying out his devilish scheme. Or was it just a war of nerves? Had he been using the fact that he was so busy as an excuse to play with her, taunting her with the prospect of what was going to happen, as a further way of punishing her for the crime of being Bronwen's niece?

But she could play at that game too, couldn't she? She could lose herself in the crowd at Fferllys, for soon the place would be crawling with even more of his staff—the place would be like Piccadilly Circus. And surely even Carlo wouldn't try anything on if it would affect his standing with his employees? And again, she began to cheer up in a perverse kind of way—there was Isabella. If she really was moving in with him—Storm herself would be safe!

Forçing herself to look on the bright side she told herself that there was going to be no way he could force her to do anything she didn't want to—he might call it passive resistance, but he could call it what he liked, no matter how cuttingly critical the tone of his voice. He was, in fact, powerless to touch her. Why, she would only have to scream for positively hordes of people to come running! A tremor of feeling shuddered through her body as a memory of his magical touch as he slowly fondled her bare skin swam before her eyes—the danger—she shuddered again—would come only from herself. If he managed to persuade her that what she felt was more than physical desire—which of course she didn't believe, she told herself fiercely—then, and only then, would there be a danger of giving in to the art of his seduction.

But she didn't feel more than bodily attraction, did she? How could she when he was such a brute? He himself agreed that love was rubbish and didn't really exist except in somebody's fevered imagination. And all she had to do to convince herself fully that this was right was to remind herself of poor Bronwen and all her pointless years of fidelity to Griff. That didn't exactly prove that love didn't exist—but it did prove that it was mad to give in to the power of the imagination.

Feeling more cheerful than she had felt for some time,

she went to the wall phone that Carlo had had put in for his chef, and punched out the number for David's office. When she got through, she felt pleased to hear his voice, despite what Carlo had said about him—there were worse traits than dullness, she concluded.

'I can't talk now, Storm, I have a client with me——'

'I wondered if, if I offered to cook you a meal in the new kitchen, you'd care to drive up to Fferylls after work?'

'Surely. I'd love to—say about sevenish?'

She was just about to ring off when she felt rather than heard the presence of someone behind her. With the phone clutched to the side of her face, she spun in time to see Carlo unwind from a position in the doorway where he had obviously been listening in to her conversation, and come sauntering into the room towards her.

'So this is what you're doing, taking time off to make secret assignations with your lover?' he mocked, eyes glittering over her flushed face as he noted her confusion.

She heard David's voice tweet against the side of her face. Carlo came right up to her and took the phone slowly out of her nerveless fingers and replaced it on its rest on the wall.

B-b-but I was in the middle of a call——'

His reply was simply to lift her chin and pull her powerfully into his arms, lips ravaging her own with such unwavering insistence that she could only submit, while all the time hating the way in which her earlier feeling of calm was obliterated in the turbulent emotions that one irresistible show of superior force could bring about. She was powerless to fight him.

'It looks as if I just can't keep my hands off you,' he murmured huskily into her hair, echoing her own feelings. 'I think I'm going to give the workmen the rest of the day off so we can have a little privacy.'

She could hear the hammering of her own heart-beats at the prospect of the whole house becoming silent as the workmen installing the rest of the central heating deserted the place.

But she was safe as long as there were other people around. Staggering back against the kitchen table she put up a hand to ward him off. 'It's only physical desire, Carlo,' she told him thickly. 'It doesn't mean anything. It's the same—it's like having a good meal or drink——' she faltered.

His reply was to dig both his hands deep into the rich tresses of her hair and drag her up close to him again. There was a look of unfathomable intensity on his face when he spoke. 'You've had the wrong lovers if that's what you believe, little girl,' he told her, speaking in a smoky, emotion-charged voice. 'I'll have to teach you something that will prevent you ever having that blasé, unimaginably wrong-headed attitude ever again. Real love-making will ruin you for cheap imitations for the rest of your life.'

'But you don't agree with love, you said so yourself,' she argued back weakly.

'I "agree" with love, as you put it—but not with that sentimental twaddle that says you love David. You feel sorry for him, you might even like him, but it's not love and never will be.'

Because she knew in her heart that he was right, she could only gaze in speechless dismay at his handsome face, longing to surrender to him, but fearing the inevitable parting that would follow.

He switched suddenly to his brisk business-efficient tone and ordered, 'Get me a cup of coffee, will you? I'm busy and you've obviously got all the time in the world.'

Shrugging, as if the pain his manner caused didn't exist, she went over to the machine and watched as it perked and the cup filled with black coffee.

'Milk, sir?' she asked sarcastically.

'No, but I'm glad you asked,' he went on. 'It should save some embarrassment when we find ourselves breakfasting in a hotel together for the first time.'

'That'll be the day,' she snorted.

'Won't it!' He was watching her intently, his face suddenly strained. 'There was another reason for seeking you out.' He took something from his back pocket and held it out to her. Puzzled, she took it, conscious as she did so of the narrow-eyed scrutiny to which he was subjecting her.

'Tickets!' she responded in surprise. 'Tickets to Paris! Who are they for?'

'I found them on your drawing board, so presumably they're intended for you?'

'Me?'

'Very good,' he observed. 'You ought to go on the stage. You expressed just the right element of surprise there to fool anyone who didn't know you as well as I'm beginning to.'

'But they can't be for me——' Suddenly she felt herself colour violently as a wild idea struck her.

'There's a note about oysters scrawled on the cover of your drawing pad too.' He eyed her coolly, confirming her suspicions. 'As they're popularly believed to have certain aphrodisiac qualities, it doesn't take much imagination to guess what the purpose of a trip to gay Paree would be for, does it?' Suddenly his face lost its bantering good humour and like a storm-cloud his smile was obliterated as he gripped her painfully by both shoulders and began to shake her violently.

'Who is he, Storm? Which one of my employees imagines he's made it to first base?' His expression darkened even more as he added, 'Or perhaps he's already got what he wanted and this is a thank you for services rendered? Well?—Well?'

'How can you think such a thing? I hate you!' She was shouting now, outraged by what he was suggesting and whipped to a fury by the brutal way he was holding her. 'I hate you! I hate you! Take your horrible hands off me!'

His face seemed to be suffused with jealousy. 'So it's the outraged virgin act again, is it? Don't you think it's a little late for that?' He gave her one last hard shake and she thought he was going to strike her, but instead he gritted his teeth, glowering, 'To think I nearly fell for that one—seeing you so pale and fragile surrounded by spring flowers in your room the day I came back! I'd been having a radical change of heart while I was away, and the way you looked seemed to confirm that I was right to rethink things—what a fool I nearly made of myself! You little bitch, Storm! How you must be secretly laughing up your sleeve—you've got what you wanted, haven't you? The free run of Fferllys—handed to you on a plate! You're made in the same mould as your scheming adulteress aunt——' He seemed to be about to raise his hand to strike her when she cried out, flinching back against the table with her hands over her face to protect herself.

'No!' he was panting. 'You won't drive me to do something that would make me end up despising myself. You'll never have that kind of power over me—you won't win every hand. But you've blown your cover—these tickets are proof of what you're really like underneath the innocent, little-girl-lost façade, and I was right in my first estimation, nothing you can say will change my opinion now!'

He began to move menacingly close to her, making her stagger back as far as she could get from out of his reach before she suddenly found herself bumping hard against the wall, her retreat stopped. But he came on again, and she gazed up at him, white-faced.

'What are you going to do, Carlo?' she demanded hoarsely, staring in wide-eyed horror as he loomed over her.

'Wh-what are——' But one hand snaked out to finger the side of her neck as her words trailed hopelessly away, and as she flinched at his touch he emitted a humourless chuckle. 'Don't tremble so, my darling,' he intoned ironically. 'I'm not going to do anything here so long as you tell me who so thoughtfully tried to provide you with a weekend in Paris.'

'I—I don't know,' she stammered, blushing at the lie and guiltily averting her face.

The strength of his fingers forced her to look up at him.

'You don't *know*? You make it sound worse than it surely is. Are there so many men willing to pay for your favours?' His fingers pressed cruelly against the muscles at the back of her neck. 'Well?' he prompted. 'Can't you answer?'

Again she tried to twist her head to avoid his gaze and again he exerted a little extra pressure. But this time when he spoke his voice was taut with impatience at her refusal to give him the name he wanted.

'Don't try to protect him, whoever he is. I only have to make a couple of guesses to find him out, but I want the satisfaction of hearing you say his name. Come on, Storm. You know I know who he is, just say it for me.'

Her head fluttered from side to side like a bird in a snare in a vain effort to escape, but his other hand gripped tightly round her waist, pinning her helplessly back against the wall.

'Come on, Storm, say it. Why won't you tell me? Are you afraid of what else I'll discover? I'll only have to ask him. Even you know that. Nobody's going to risk losing his job to protect you. I'll hear the full story before the day's out from one source or another. Now, come on, stop being so damned obstinate!' He was behaving like a man possessed by a jealous rage, and it didn't make sense. It couldn't be jealousy that was driving him to try to prise an answer from her—jealousy stemmed from a fear of losing a loved one and he certainly didn't love her, not after all he had said to her. She shuddered.

'Take your horrible hands off me! I'm not going to say

anything until you let me go!' she cried in bewilderment.

Her protests were a waste of breath. 'Tell me,' he insisted through gritted teeth, 'I haven't got all day.' Gradually he increased the pressure on the back of her neck as if to show he really meant it.

Storm's mouth had gone dry but she gazed up at him defiantly, her face flushed and furious, overriding her physical fear of him. 'You can't bully me, Carlo. It won't work! You should know that by now!'

'Of course!' he laughed shortly. 'There's only one method that works with you, even at a time like this. How could I have forgotten?'

Even as it dawned on her what method he meant, his mouth came down hard on hers, crushing the breath from her and bringing their two bodies up in violent, suddenly electric contact that made the blood pulse visibly at her temples and the small cry of protest she made change to one of hateful surrender as her two hands came up, not to push him away as her mind told her she should, but to draw him down, bringing her own body arching up to meet him. It was an embrace that seemed to go on and on in steadily mounting intensity, both of them driven by an anger that fed their desire, until their heart-beats seemed to match in ever-increasing speed, the throb of blood mirroring and mingling on a steady crescendo of ecstasy that was like a symphony of desire carrying them both on into another world.

A sharp feminine cry from the direction of the doorway caused Carlo to lift his head abruptly, and Storm just had time to see him staring blearily at a figure standing there before a single name sent her recoiling in dismay at the sight of Isabella stalking, head erect, into the kitchen.

The haughty face registered bewilderment rather than the anger Storm expected, but the enormity of what she had done, surrendering yet again to Carlo's superior will, made her cower back, red-faced with embarrassment, as the older woman looked her coolly up and down.

Her glance then flicked icily to Carlo who was still holding Storm in his arms and making no attempt to release her.

'I wanted a word with you, Carlo—perhaps when you're free?' she asked, arching her pencil-thin brows. Then she turned swiftly and walked out without further comment. Storm discovered that she was trembling with a mixture of shame at betraying her desire so openly to Carlo and humiliation at having her self-betrayal witnessed by a rival—and one with a special claim on Carlo's attentions.

Because she felt that what had happened had been largely her fault—her fault for attracting Carlo's desire in the first place, and her fault for not saying no and meaning it just now—her immediate impulse was to apologise to him for causing what could only erupt as trouble between him and his fiancée, but she managed to stifle the word in time as she saw him step back from her with a look of shrivelling contempt on his face.

'Thanks a lot, Storm. That'll teach me to keep my hands off you at work, won't it?'

'Yes, perhaps it will!' she replied in a defiant voice. 'I never asked you to kiss me——'

'But you sure as hell didn't put up much of a resistance when I did——' He looked almost amused as he gazed down at her flushed face and still-parted soft pink lips. 'In fact you look ready for kissing again——' he murmured, coming closer.

'No!' She shrank back. 'How can you? Isabella must be so hurt and angry.'

'Isabella?' He looked mystified for a moment. 'Oh—Isabella. Did you think she was shocked? She's seen worse scenes than this. She'll get over it——'

'You callous brute——' She pushed inefectually at his broad shoulders without much result as he at once brought his lips down to her own, but before kissing her he murmured, 'You nearly made me forget why I was doing this to you, you little witch. Now come on, be a good girl, was it Raimondo?'

'What—? Who——?' Storm shivered. She too had for a moment forgotten why he was inflicting this treatment on her but now it came back to her, not, however, before the answer to his question was clearly affirmed by the expression in her eyes.

'Fast work!' he commented drily. 'You realise he's married, of course?'

'Y-yes, he told me,' she faltered, 'and he told me about his three children——'

'He must have guessed they would present no obstacle to the morals of a girl like yourself—do you often have affairs with married men? Don't you ever feel a qualm of conscience at the lies and the deceit involved?' he demanded contemptuously.

The cruelty of his accusation made Storm speechless for a minute and he took it as a sign of indifference. Gripping her so that she winced, he told her, 'I'm going to make you care!' His fingers bit more deeply into her soft flesh.

'Don't Carlo—please let me go——'

'Don't Carlo,' he mimicked, dragging her against him. 'I'm going to make you feel for once in your life—so don't give me that look of calculated indifference! You're going to feel and hurt and bleed as other people do.' He ran a finger lingeringly down the side of her neck. 'I'm going to make you face up to the responsibility for your actions. You're going to know what it's like to suffer the pain of being married to a faithless husband. Storm,' his fingers bit into her flesh again, 'there's only one way to do it. I'm going to marry you!'

CHAPTER EIGHT

STORM didn't know whether she was dreaming or not. After he had left her, presumably with the intention of mollifying his justifiably upset fiancée, his words seemed so unlikely that she had to kick herself to make sure she was still awake.

How could he say he was going to marry her when he hated her so much? His motive should be love, not hatred. And did he expect her simply to acquiesce, knowing how little he really cared for her?

Her nerves tautened in a spiral of panic and anger at the thought of how she would be torn apart if she was forced to endure the intimacy of the marriage bed while knowing that when he wasn't with her he was making love to other women. Could he guess how this would savage her to the soul? With sickening insight she saw that she wanted his motive for marrying her to be love—the sort of love, she shuddered, that, despite everything that had happened, had somehow taken over her heart. This new realisation felt as if scales were falling from her eyes. Yes, of course she desired him. But was it simple physical lust that made everything about him seem so dear? Her mind spun crazily, searching for an avenue of escape. It couldn't be love—yet it seemed all too clear now. And how he would crow in triumph if he guessed! She had fallen into his hands like an over-ripe peach, she lashed herself, and now she was suffering because he was winding his magic thread even more tightly around her heart.

Dear God, she thought, my body aches for him night and day. Looking back over the past few weeks she could see clearly now why she had been in such emotional turmoil. I can't eat, I can't sleep, I can't work, I can't even think straight, she thought feverishly. How much worse will it be after we make love? She felt as if she had no control over her mind—he had invaded her thoughts with insulting ease from the moment they had met, as if she had been doing nothing with her life but wait for him, waiting for him alone. Nothing, surely, could be further from the truth? She hadn't forgotten, had she, the years of painful solitude Bronwen had endured because of Griff? Now his son had stormed into her life like a conquering hero come to claim his bounty—he had warned her he wanted her home, her livelihood, her body and her soul. But the first thing he had commandeered was her mind—it had been filled with thoughts of him from the beginning. She despised her own weakness, the lack of control that prevented her from getting on with her own life. But he had invaded her soul, lodging himself in a place that she had always been careful to keep empty.

Dear God, she moaned, how can I escape? And if I can't escape, how can I conceal from him the extent of his triumph?

She was given no opportunity to find out what was behind his glib proposal, for throughout the rest of the day he seemed to be in a constant state of busyness, and though she caught sight of him at intervals in the distance, now with Raimondo, now with Isabella, she couldn't judge from the way they looked what the nature of their conversation might be—they all looked as if there was nothing on their minds other than the completion of the final stage of the renovation of Fferllys.

At least she had got the privacy of her own studio again, though his brief case and a couple of files were still lying scattered over the desk.

Luce popped her head in half-way through the

afternoon, agog with excitement on being invited, along with all the others, to a dinner party to celebrate the completion of the work.

'Just think, Fferllys is going to be the H.Q. for an international company. And I've always thought it was such a little backwater!'

'Maybe now you'll decide not to seek fame and fortune in London after all?' smiled Storm, aware of the teenager's ambition and striving to appear on the surface exactly like her normal self.

'I'm not so sure about that—but it's a thought!'

'Your mum would be pleased if you stayed—not to mention Hughie.'

Luce grinned. 'You've got a point. Still, who knows!' She went back down with Storm's empty coffee cup, whistling cheerfully as she tripped lightly down the spiral staircase.

There was no joy in Storm's contemplation of the dinner celebration ahead—it would just have to be something to be faced when the time came. Thoughts of what Isabella must be thinking made her cringe inside.

David arrived as arranged at seven o'clock. She had been watching out for him from the high window of her bedroom with a feeling that she was barricaded in. First she saw the women wending their way down to the village, then Carlo's assistants in their cars or on bikes, and finally Carlo and Isabella leaving together as usual. They seemed the best of friends, Storm noted with a dart of jealousy, and she wondered what tale he had spun the dark-haired woman about the incident in the kitchen that morning. It must have been a good one, she judged, for Isabella seemed both shrewd and sophisticated, and she wouldn't have thought it would be an easy task to pull the wool over her eyes. She had begun to disbelieve his decision to marry her—Isabella would surely not behave with such serenity if she had been told that her fiancé had transferred his affections to someone else? Though perhaps Carlo had outlined in every detail his motives for doing so? Perhaps Isabella felt secure in the assurance that she would continue to be his mistress? Perhaps their continued association was destined to be an integral part of the whole plot?

Knowing her face must look unnaturally pale despite her careful use of pearly pink blusher, she made her way down to meet David and reached the bottom stairs just as he came in through the door. In the shadows her imagination played a strange trick and she felt dizzy at her image of Carlo, of how he had stood against the opposite wall, watching her silently with such a strange, unfathomable expression in his blue eyes, after kissing her that time when Phyllis had nearly discovered them.

Her hands felt like ice as David, more insubstantial than the figure in her imagination, took them both in greeting.

'No heat on in the place, Storm? Isn't the central heating working yet?'

She nodded. 'Yes, come into the new sitting-room. There's a solid fuel stove in there—it's very pretty. It's a copy of one of those eighteenth century French ones——' she chattered, turning quickly to forestall his affectionate peck on the cheek.

There was no sign of Raimondo in the room and she recalled that throughout the day she had watched out for him in the hope of getting a chance to have a quiet word, but someone told her he had gone out in the car about mid-afternoon, and so far she hadn't seen him come back.

David was suitably impressed by the improvements that had been carried out and made appreciative noises when he stepped into the warmth of the new sitting-room.

'It's all certainly changed since Llewellyn took over. When's the final completion date?'

'Officially on Friday, if they can manage it. We're

celebrating then anyway, whatever happens. You will come, won't you, David?' she asked anxiously. It suddenly seemed very important to have the reassuring hand of David to hold while Carlo and Isabella entertained the staff.

'If you really want me to——' he replied carefully.

'Of course I do, why shouldn't I?' she responded at once.

He squeezed her arm, 'OK. I'll escort you. But you don't have to look as if we shall be entering the lion's den! . . . Where shall we be dining by the way?'

'The Feathers . . . He's booked the whole restaurant.'

David looked a trifle disappointed and couldn't help saying, 'That's a pity. I was hoping to save The Feathers for a rather more intimate dinner for just the two of us in the not too distant future.'

He came to sit beside her on the new beige leather suite and took her still, cold hand in his own. His grey eyes looked earnestly into hers and he went on gruffly. 'I know you can't be seeing anybody else because you spend every evening with me these days—so I suppose it's a sign that your brief infatuation with that other chap you mentioned a few weeks ago is now over.' He dropped his glance bashfully then added, 'I've been biding my time in the hope that it'll all blow over—and now that it looks as if it might have, it seems like the right time for us to start thinking of putting our relationship on to a slightly more serious footing——'

'Oh, David.' She looked moved, while concealing the fact that in reality her thoughts were thrown into turmoil again, and he was sufficiently encouraged to put an arm loosely around her shoulders and gaze soulfully into her eyes, saying, 'Don't let's say any more right now. I don't want either of us to rush into anything.'

A bubble of hysterical laughter fought to be released and she automatically bent her head, resting it on his shoulder in order to keep it down. It wasn't that she was laughing at David, though this might have been what he would have thought if he had heard a laugh at such a moment, it was more like the shock, that break in the armour plating round her inmost feelings preventing her from confiding in any one, that made her feel that she was on the edge of losing control. Until now she had thought of David as her best friend, but his clear intention was to become something more—and by doing so the natural exchange of confidences would automatically be censored. Sorry at losing him in his former role and in a state of confusion at the added responsibility to protect his tenderer feelings now they had been declared, she could only press her face into the comforting tweed of his sports jacket and allow him to stroke her hair with the slightly bemused air of someone who has unexpectedly found himself embracing a tiger, while her emotions played havoc with her equilibrium.

The sun, framed in the pencil-shaped windows, was setting in long golden slants across the crisp white carpet, and it must have accentuated their two shapes sitting locked in each other's arms within its golden embrace, for a cynical voice from the doorway broke the silence with, 'Quite a picture! What a pity I haven't got a camera!'

With a tremor she watched as Carlo strode casually into the room and spread his lithe length over the sofa opposite.

'And what should we entitle it? "Love's Dream" or "The Follies of the Heart"—or have you any other suggestions? What about——'

'Carlo!' she exclaimed warningly, every nerve alive at this unexpected onslaught on her senses.

David, who sprung back as if caught in a more compromising position, protested, 'Dash it all, Carlo——' and was presumably about to offer a mild reproof when he caught the look in Carlo's eye and decided that his apparent mockery had been intended as a joke all along.

'Just lending my shoulder to cry on——' he muttered gruffly, picking up Storm's limp hand in a gesture that held an element of defiance in it.

'And very capable looking shoulders they are, too,' Carlo observed in a tone so light that only Storm guessed at the mockery it concealed.

She eyed them both suspiciously then. 'I didn't know you two knew each other,' she offered, puzzled by David's use of Carlo's name in that fairly familiar fashion.

David had the grace to look uncomfortable as he said with patent insincerity, 'Oh, didn't I mention it, darling?'

'I decided to deliver a copy of the Deeds in person when I first came up here,' Carlo broke in. 'It seemed a good idea to take the opportunity to have lunch together while I was making up my mind whether to settle here. David's firm happens to be one of the oldest in the county—what he couldn't tell me about the locality—and the people,' he added with a brief darkening of his eyes, 'wouldn't be worth knowing.'

Beside her, Storm felt David give a start of pleasure at the compliment and she marvelled at the ease with which Carlo could get everyone eating out of his hand. Looking at the lines of ruthless confidence on his face she could imagine the cold-blooded way he would set out to discover everything he needed to know before deciding to establish his H.Q. at Fferllys. A lunch here, a drink there. Piecing together his little bits of information like a sleuth before committing himself. He simply exuded a hard-headed, practical confidence in his own judgment that made David look like the college boy he had until recently been. She could also see how her presence at Fferllys had been the fly in the ointment for him at the beginning and how David's rather prudish outlook would have coloured everything he said about Bronwen.

'You aren't cross with me, are you, darling? It honestly slipped my mind,' David told her, making her cringe for him as Carlo listened with a small, ambiguous smile playing round his full lips.

As she met those blue eyes a mocking light came into them which David was too self-absorbed to notice, and she trembled inwardly as she was exposed to the searching glance that travelled over her, a glance that was narrow, hard and sardonic. Then it turned into a slow, sensual appraisal, wandering over her form without shame, making her squirm uneasily at the thought of what might happen next—or what might have happened if David hadn't been sitting safely by her side.

Aware that her feelings towards both men had changed drastically, she acknowledged the fact that just to look at Carlo made her tingle all over, whereas the pressure of David's leg against her own was an irritation.

She edged further along the sofa to establish a less intimate space between them and noted that David didn't even notice. Carlo did, however, his eyes becoming brilliant with some private thought.

'Don't let me disturb you both,' he remarked, bringing himself athletically to his feet.

'Stay by all means—that's all right, isn't it, Storm?' encouraged David as if it was up to him and obviously eager to further a business contact. To Storm it seemed that he was almost grovelling in his insistence that Carlo stay and it made Storm angry that he should play into Carlo's hands.

'Actually I have a few business matters to attend to, that's why I had to come back tonight. But if you really mean it—I'll join you in a night-cap later on?' He paused. 'I don't want to butt in if you're planning on having a romantic evening *à deux* . . .' He adopted a look of exaggerated concern that had the effect of making David insist, and Carlo could scarcely conceal the glint of amusement in his eyes as he caught sight of Storm's furious expression.

When he had left them to work next door in his office, she turned on David in a fury.

'Can't you see what a snake he is?' she demanded. 'You played right into his hands!'

'What are you talking about? Snake? Carlo?'

'Oh, you're so *stupid*!' she cried in exasperation.

The look of bewilderment on his face only added to her irritation. His jaw visibly dropped at the sight of her angry face. 'It's only a drink, for heaven's sake,' he protested mildly. 'Where's the harm in that?'

'Because—oh, nothing! What's the point?' She could hardly explain all the ramifications to him and instead relapsed into a sulky silence, dreading the moment when she would have to endure Carlo's lazy appraisal while he had his 'night-cap'.

'I know what it is,' David said eventually putting out a tentative hand to cover one of hers, 'you wanted a nice cosy evening as he said, *à deux*. I'm sorry, darling, I didn't think.'

Storm sighed. At least it was an ego-saving excuse and why should poor David be needlessly hurt by the flak that was flying, innocent bystander that he was?

With a feeling of inevitability she settled back into the crook of his arm and flicked the automatic control on the television.

'There's that foreign affairs programme you wanted to catch, David. Had you forgotten?'

Carlo hadn't forgotten them, however. He made it his business to come in and out several times in the course of the evening on the pretext of looking up different things in the pile of reference books that were waiting to be unpacked and properly shelved as soon as the book rack was up. Storm had the suspicion that it was his way of showing he was in charge, of dictating the situation, keeping an eye on her as he had always managed to do one way or another. It made her smart but she didn't feel she could count on David to back her up should she try to have a show-down.

How she could wipe the smiles off both their faces if she announced that Carlo had stated his intention to marry her! Restraining the impulse she at least took the opportunity, on one of Carlo's forays amongst the books, to ask him about Raimondo.

'He's left,' he told her bluntly, standing up to his full height with a book in his hand whose pages he turned even as he spoke to her.

'Left?' she queried, shooting a glance at David, who, however, was quite absorbed by some political discussion.

'Yes,' replied Carlo, turning and making towards the door. He paused with his hand on the door knob. 'I sent him back to South America. It's safer there for him. Sorry.' With a narrow smile he went out, leaving Storm to experience a pang of guilt at the thought that she must be the one to blame for this latest development—Carlo, true to his word, obviously did not approve of his staff playing around, or even seeming to, in this case.

Storm felt a qualm of regret that she hadn't made more effort to ram home the truth when Carlo had first questioned her about the tickets. It wasn't fair on Raimondo. She must accidentally have encouraged him into believing that she would willingly accompany him on a trip to Paris. Goodness knows what lascivious ambitions had led him to go out and buy two tickets. Surely he couldn't believe she was a girl like that? What had she done? How had she done it? Or was it a reflection of his boss's attitude to her—had it somehow rubbed off, sullying her reputation unjustifiably amongst his staff?

Waves of shame, mingled with anger at the injustice of such an impression, washed up and down her body. It *must* be her fault, she castigated herself silently, for no one would go to all that expense without good cause, would they?

'David, I'm not a flirt, am I?' She shook his arm to distract him from the television.

'Sorry, darling, what was that?'

She sighed and repeated the question.

'Of course not,' he replied stoutly, 'if by that you mean a feather-brained little idiot with only one aim in life.'

She sighed again, this time in exasperation. 'Would you actually *know*?' she demanded crossly as he turned back to the screen.

He swung his head at once. 'I should say so. It has been known, you know.'

'What has?'

'Well you know——'

'I don't know, David. Why can't you stop beating about the bush?'

'Well, girls have been known to flutter the old eyelashes at a chap, you know.'

'Your older woman?' she probed cruelly.

'Dash it all, Storm, I told you that in strictest confidence. I don't want it thrown back in my face all the time. Look here——' He took hold of her by the upper arm and held it tightly as he spoke. 'You're in a funny mood. What's up? I've a right to know.'

'It's just Rai,' she heard herself saying, before she could stop herself. 'Carlo says he's sent him back to South America.'

'So?' he probed, peering closely into her face in the failing light from the setting sun.

'Well——' she paused, unsure how to go on, then she blurted, 'I think it may have had something to do with me. I mean, it might be my fault——'

'*Your* fault?'

Briefly Storm wondered if David had always had this irritating way of cross-questioning people. 'Yes,' she went on, 'It must be because of something that happened . . .'

'Come on, old girl, tell Uncle David what you've been up to,' he encouraged. Then a thought seemed to strike him and she watched his face redden as he blurted with a sudden gust of insight, 'You don't mean to say that—he's the other man?'

'The other—oh, no! . . . Raimondo? No, not really! I mean——' Blushing, she realised what he meant, but her protestations only seemed to confirm his mistaken assumption that he had guessed the object of her secret love and he held her hand very tighlty as he probed further. 'If he's not the man, why should Carlo send him away? Why should you come to the conclusion that it's your fault?'

'Oh, it was just some silly misunderstanding about some tickets to Paris——' As she said it, she realised how bad it must sound. Now David was determined to get to the bottom of the whole thing.

'What tickets? Whose were they? Why Paris? Did he intend to take you with him? . . . Is that what it's all about? . . . But he's a married man, Storm, as well as—dash it all, I mean to say——' Shocked dismay and a look of hurt disbelief vied in David's face for supremacy. He rose to his feet and began to pace in front of the television, a grim expression coming into his face as he gravely considered the rights and wrongs of the situation as he now saw it. 'I can't say I'm not shocked,' he muttered, 'but no doubt there's a simple enough explanation for it. Well,' he swivelled to face her, 'are you going to tell me what it's all about?'

Just then Carlo came back again. He was smiling—hypocritically, thought Storm—but when he saw David pacing up and down, his assessment that something was wrong showed in the narrowing of his eyes and the alert raising of his dark head. Instead of this making him back tactfully out of the room as any reasonable person would have done, raged Storm inwardly, his smile merely broadened and he lounged across to an arm-chair and sprawled in it with the air of a man having just completed a marathon.

'I could certainly do with a drink,' he remarked, obviously, eyeing the drinks cabinet. To Storm's disgust David forgot his pacing and went over to 'do the honours'. His suspicion that she might have been up to something behind his back with Carlo's right-hand man made him eye her with a certain puzzled coldness even as he handed her a glass of her favourite drink, but, relieved that at least Carlo's presence would put a stop to any cross-questioning David might have felt tempted to indulge in, she set her drink down carefully on a side table saying ironically, 'This is cosy. Shall we have a game of Scrabble?'

'I really ought to be getting back soon,' David remarked dourly.

Carlo didn't make any comment and it struck Storm with the force of an electric shock that within less than an hour she could be entirely alone in the house and helplessly at the mercy of the wolfishly smiling man sitting opposite her. The same thought had obviously struck him at the same time and his smile widened. Storm blanched.

'No, you may as well stay the night, David. The guest-rooms are ready now,' she said hurriedly.

'Don't you have to get into work early tomorrow morning? suggested Carlo with a significant glance at the clock.

David looked undecided.

'Better to drive back down that dreadful road in broad daylight than risk it tonight.' Storm touched his arm. 'Do stay, David. I'm always staying at your place and it'll give me a chance to repay some of your hospitality.'

'Yes, that's only fair, isn't it?' Carlo agreed in an unexpected volte-face and with a sardonic smile added,

'Storm does hate not being able to repay her debts.'

'Well, if it's all right——' David weakly acquiesced, obviously overcome that everything should be decided for him in so cut and dried a manner.

Storm was still glowering at Carlo for his last remark when they all eventually decided to turn in.

'Easily persuaded, isn't he?' Carlo murmured in her ear as he prepared to say good night. David was fussing about not having a toothbrush but Storm found a new one and showed him where the new bathrooms were, choosing some clean bedlinen and generally trying to make amends. When she came out of the spare room Carlo was walking past the door.

'He's really very decisive,' she felt constrained to defend him. 'It's you. Most people can't take your constant bullying.'

'But *you* can?' he chuckled softly. 'Dear Storm, you may think you've won a round tonight. But don't forget there are several more rounds to go before the match is won.'

Her outraged gasp sent him off smiling in the direction of his own suite. 'Don't forget to lock your door, darling——' he paused, for one last taunt, 'or alternatively, don't bother—if you really are bluffing!'

His extra insult gave her the opportunity to come back with a hiss of anger and she spun back to face him. Keeping her voice low, because David was in the bathroom next to them gargling and rattling around, she hissed, 'The trouble with you, Carlo Llewellyn, is that you were born with a silver spoon in your mouth and you think all you have to do is click you fingers and the world jumps into line. Well for once in your life you've met your match!' Her vehemence almost failed her when she noticed the way his lazy glance travelled suggestively up the length of her taut and angry body, resting with special interest on her breasts that were rising and falling rapidly with the force of her anger. 'And don't look at me like that!' she clipped. 'I'm not like you think. There must be some explanation for Rai buying those tickets. It was crazy of you to send him away——' She paused, biting her lip. 'Has he lost his job?' she queried on a slightly doubtful note.

'He's too valuable to lose over a minor peccadillo,' he replied curtly, his face losing its bantering smile. 'I sent him back for the sake of his marriage, not to punish you by denying you a sexy weekend. And anyway, you needn't worry—I'll make it up to you soon and you can come to Paris with me instead . . . I'll give you more than *you* can handle!'

'Huh, boasting again!' she flashed, taking a step back as she taunted him with a toss of her long hair.

'Are you calling me a liar?' he demanded dangerously, matching her pace back with one forward of his own.

Their eyes fenced rapidly, only the sound of David pulling the plug in the washbasin and obviously reaching the end of his bedtime preparations bringing a halt to any further developments.

'Time to say good night, Storm, pleasant dreams—dream of me!'

'I thought you said "pleasant dreams"?' she jibed.

She wasn't quick enough to avoid the one hand that shot out pulling her towards him by one thick strand of long hair. 'You always want to have the last word, don't you, darling?' he murmured threateningly in her ear. 'You'd better make the most of your opportunities because when I get you in private you're not going to have time to talk at all.'

'Threats, threats, threats,' she couldn't help goading.

'That's it——' his lips crushed down and she felt her bones turn to liquid. Then before she could mutter a protest, he had released her and swivelled towards his suite.

For what seemed like an age she stared after him. Her lips burning, her body tense with the unrequited yearning to experience the full power of his touch.

'But he doesn't love me,' she cried into her pillow that night. 'And I shall only be playing into his hands if I let him know how I feel.' Even as she drifted off to sleep she recognised that if he was serious about his crazy plan to marry her, she was incapable of saying 'no'. She felt like someone condemned but she knew she was doing it to herself—that if she tried hard enough she could get up and walk away from him for surely it was only lack of determination that made her feel she could deny nothing he would ever ask of her?

CHAPTER NINE

FFERLLYS was a place transformed by the end of the week. All the deadlines for the conversion of Carlo's new H.Q. had been met—the only thing that remained to be done now was the redecoration of the bedrooms in the old domestic quarters. The delay here was due to the fact that Storm simply hadn't had the heart, or the time, to get around to going through all Bronwen's old things and turfing out whatever she didn't want to keep.

Carlo strode briskly into the studio half-way through the morning. He looked busy, his black hair rumpled boyishly and his shirt collar open, tie askew, and, not mentioning the previous night, he told her how pleased he was with the way everything was bang on schedule, then he frowned. 'I see you haven't bothered to clear those three rooms for the decorators,' he remarked. 'They're having to come back next week and I've asked them to finish off your room and—er—the other two . . .' He paused as if reluctant to mention Bronwen's name.

'Don't look at me like that!' flared Storm. 'I've told you I'll clear Bronwen's rooms when I have time. I'm in the middle of the work for Nick—it's far more important than playing house for you!'

'Is it?' he demanded harshly. 'Is it really?'

There was a hollow silence in which they both glared aggressively at one another. His face twisted with something that could easily have been mistaken for pain before he managed to blank it off.

'Why not get one of your underlings to do it?' Storm croaked eventually, refusing to drop her glance.

Carlo's brow furrowed. 'I would have done if I hadn't thought you'd be upset at the prospect of a complete stranger rummaging through her things.' His voice had softened.

'I've got used to having my home invaded by total strangers by now!' she snapped.

He appeared to bite back what he had been about to say and instead told her again almost gently, 'To be practical, it'd be impossible for anybody else to know what you wanted to keep, wouldn't it?'

She flushed and turned her head.

'I know it won't be a pleasant task,' he continued, 'but it's your job, Storm, and if you want the rooms decorating and refurnishing in keeping with the rest of the house, you'll simply have to face up to it.'

'Don't you come marching in here telling me what to do!' she snarled, rising from her seat. 'Who do you think you are?'

'I think you know very well who I am,' he murmured silkily, all trace of his former gentleness obliterated as he stepped forward. 'Now, are you going to do as I ask or——'

'Or what?' She shrank back against the desk. 'What *threat* are you going to make this time, Carlo Llewellyn? Will it be another of your sexy kisses, yet another instance of sexual harassment?'

'Are you trying to tell me you've found it unpleasant? Because if so you've an original way of showing it——' he replied evenly.

She blushed crimson. 'You don't imagine it's anything to do with *you*, do you?' she replied fiercely, clenching her fists. 'It's an automatic reaction when a physically attractive man kisses a girl—you surely can't imagine it actually *means* anything?'

'Obviously not,' he replied coldly. 'We're both experienced enough to know it's only lust.' The ice-blue of his eyes didn't alter when he went on, 'But that still doesn't change the fact that you obviously found it quite pleasant—I'm banking on that,' he added in an odd voice.

She shrank back although as yet he hadn't moved a step. 'I only have to scream and everyone will come running. On the other hand,' she smiled sweetly, 'perhaps I'll do that anyway—it's about time they all knew what sort of man you were——'

'Blackmail?' he raised an eyebrow. 'I thought that was unworthy of you, Storm.'

As if suddenly aware that he had work to do he gave an impatient shrug of his shoulders and turned back, dismissively, to the stairs. 'I'm too busy to stand here arguing with you. Of course I can't make you clear Bronwen's things. If you want to wallow in a lot of rubbish from the past, that's your look-out——'

'How dare you call her treasured possessions rubbish! I'll have you know most of that so-called rubbish is stuff written by *your* father,' she added grimly, 'so in that sense you may be right! Maybe it *is* rubbish. I'll call the scrap merchants myself!' She made as if to reach for the phone but he came over in two swift strides and placed one hand over hers where it momentarily rested on top of the phone.

'Look, Storm, think about it calmly, will you?' His lips compressed with impatience and without any further comment he pivoted and headed off down the stairs.

'Calmly indeed!' she muttered under her breath when he had gone. But later that morning, taking her cup of coffee with her, she mounted the narrow stairs to the second floor and pushed open the door to Bronwen's room.

No one had been in for a long time and dust had settled like a pale gauze over every surface. It looked infinitely worse than she remembered. Bronwen had never been one to throw anything away. There were sheaves of drawings from her own art school days and pile upon pile of sketches and rough ideas she had tried out over the years. Storm half-heartedly picked up a box of photographs and a large spider scuttled out. With a shudder she dropped the box back on to the floor and stood undecidedly gazing round. It was going to take ages to sort through everything, more than just a morning. Her eyes glistened. But for the hateful son of Bronwen's lover she need never come in here again. Her chin rose. Let him get someone else to do it—*she* hadn't the time.

A little posy of dried flowers was still stuck behind a hand-painted mirror, just as Bronwen had left it. What memories, now lost to time, were wound round such a keep-sake? Storm knew suddenly that she couldn't leave the job to anyone else—she owed it to Bronwen to preserve what had been important to her, just as she owed it to her to keep the design business going. With a sigh she made her way back downstairs. Some time later in the week she would have to steel herself for the task.

When she entered the kitchen where everyone was still in the process of enjoying the mid-morning coffee break, she found them discussing the evening's celebration, their hilarity clashing uneasily with her own dark thoughts. She tried to tune in to what they were saying—Carlo, she thought silently, was as much of a hit as ever—but it all seemed to be happening on another planet.

'It's nice, isn't it,' Megan was saying, 'how he's including us in all his plans. I mean, our little design workshop really has nothing to do with his side.'

'Share and share alike—it's going to be great to have a go in the sauna!' Luce commented with relish.

'Did he say that?'

'He did. And you've got the use of his typists, haven't you Storm? Photocopying, the lot.'

'Wonderful,' agreed Storm, her irony lost on these latest recruits to his fan club. It was true, he had offered her the free—free?—use of his secretarial facility, as he put it, and wanted to help her to find someone to organise her books properly. She knew it would be a boon as this was the main weakness in the way the business had been run in the past, but she couldn't help seeing it as simply another instance of his attempt to take over.

'He has no need to do it,' Phyllis was agreeing with something Gwyneth had said.

'He can't help it,' Storm broke in bitterly. 'He's the sort who just loves to be in charge.'

Phyllis looked confused by Storm's tone but thought better than to comment, merely adding, 'We're benefiting already,' she raised her new French coffee cup, 'better than stewed tea out of a mug, look you.'

'I hope this new chef's as good as he's cracked up to be—but even if he's half-way good it'll be a sight better than sandwich lunches and heated tinned soups,' Megan agreed.

Yes, everyone, thought Storm, bitterly looking round, had benefited but herself. All she had got was a crazy, threatening proposal of marriage that she wanted to treat as a joke but for some self-defeating inner purpose she hungered to turn into reality.

They went on to talk about clothes, not unusual but now with the added excitement that all their little-worn and most sophisticated gowns could be brought out of the wardrobes.

'It's about time we had an opportunity to dress up!' remarked Luce. 'There's Christmas and that's about it.'

'What are you going to wear, Storm?'

'We're planning colours so we don't clash.'

'I don't think we're going to have much choice at this late stage,' remarked Gwyneth. 'I was going to run something up but don't seem to have got round to it. For me it'll have to be the midnight blue chiffon or nothing——'

While they all teased Gwyneth that she'd be setting a new trend if she chose the latter course, Storm furrowed her brow. She hadn't given the evening a thought but obviously she couldn't let David down by appearing in any old rag. Momentarily an image of Isabella swam into her mind—her darkly vivacious looks would always be eye-catching whatever she wore.

'Storm, do you know what it's about?' Phyllis was asking her.

She came to with a start. 'Sorry, I was day-dreaming. What did you say?'

'Mr Llewellyn said there's a special reason for celebrating apart from the end of all the turmoil with the builders being over.'

A cold hand tightened on her heart. 'Special?' She shook her head doubtfully. 'He hasn't mentioned anything to me.' Her limbs were like jelly . . . surely he wouldn't have the gall to announce his intention of marrying her in public? She knew he would. It was just the sort of *fait accompli* he would relish. 'Now talk your way out of that!' she could imagine him saying with a triumphant smile.

'You all right, Storm?' She had shivered involuntarily.

'Just someone walking over my grave,' she quipped.

After she had showered that evening she sprayed herself with what was left of the expensive perfume Bronwen had given her on her last birthday and, wearing only a wrap, went to inspect the only three dresses that were at all suitable for The Feathers.

David particularly liked the pale pink chiffon with its dreamy layers of lace and high round neck. It was something she had bought for a birthday party when she was seventeen and its sweetly innocent air made her reach for it automatically, but then she stayed her hand with a sigh. She felt far too old for such an *ingénue* concoction now—it would make her feel she was playing a part in a school play. Next to it was the dress she had worn when Carlo had taken her to The Feathers on the evening they met. It wouldn't do to turn up in the same dress at the same place. So that left only a dress she had bought in the sales last summer. It was a narrow, clingy button-through silk in stark black. It was backless, with a tiny boned bodice that could be made even more revealing by unfastening the tiny black buttons at neck and hem. She had never worn it because when she had made her first appearance in it, ready for a Golf Club dinner with David, he had blushingly asked her if she thought it was quite suitable for the occasion intended.

Crossly she had gone upstairs to change, throwing it into the back of a cupboard and until now thinking no more of it. After a quick iron it would do perfectly. David would just have to accept it. Quickly slipping it on just to make sure it still fitted, she cinched in the wide matching belt to its tightest notch, and went to stand in front of the mirror. It did wonderful things for her shape, modelling her breasts with its subtle arrangement of darts, skimming her hips flatteringly below the provocatively narrow waist, and when she experimentally unbuttoned the last two buttons to make it easier to take her customary swinging strides, and rather daringly undid the top button to reveal even more of the pearly skin of her breasts, she could easily see that David had had a point. But for the Golf Club she had been going to wear it fastened as well as having thrown a wrap loosely round her shoulders. David was just a stick-in-the mud, there were no two ways about it. For The Feathers it would do very nicely!

Moving this way and that to view it from every side she was mesmerised by the images it conjured up—she could almost feel Carlo's long brown fingers sliding between the silky top and feathering sensuously over her breasts held only by the delicate boning in the bodice, as one by one he slowly and languorously began to unfasten each button until . . . Hastily she fastened it up, slipping on a pair of high-heeled sandals as she did so, to add height to her diminutive figure. David would be there to protect her tonight and Carlo was hardly likely to try to take advantage of her with crowds of employees present.

Brushing her naturally lustrous hair with long energetic strokes, she piled it up in glossy curls on top of her head, added delicate filigree silver ear-rings and a thin antique chain, then slipped a silky wrap about her bare shoulders.

She took particular care over her make-up, not with the intention of rivalling Isabella—but merely trying to accentuate the misty violet of her eyes that contrasted so effectively with the lustre of her hair and the fragile Dresden pink and white of her skin. Pleased with the result, and hoping that David wouldn't be stuffy about her dress, she made her way down to the sitting-room to wait for him.

She had been there several minutes and was beginning to worry that they were going to be late when the tall shape of a man clad in a dinner-jacket loomed in the doorway, making her jump.

'I thought you'd already left,' she scowled from her place by the window.

His black-fringed blue eyes glittered as they raked deliberately over the provocative curves revealed by the black silk dress and he told her roughly, 'There was a phone call for you while you were in the shower.'

Despite the rough manner he looked disconcertingly handsome and sophisticated in his formal white jacket with his black tie as yet unknotted hanging down over his dazzling white shirt. His rugged, masculine good looks were enhanced by the gleam of his dark tan against the white shirt.

Steadying herself, Storm raised her eyebrows imperiously.

'From David,' he replied.

A spasm of anxiety ran through her. 'Oh?'

There was something ambivalent about the way he said the name that should have warned her to expect the worst.

'He sends his apologies about tonight,' Carlo smiled.

Storm could only stare. 'What's wrong with him?' she demanded icily.

'Nothing much, as far as I could tell. He has another engagement, I understand.'

'But he can't have!' she blurted before she could stop herself.

'I'm afraid he may by now suspect that there's something between us, Storm. It's only right that he should know——'

'You mean you've——!' A hand flew to her mouth. 'Carlo Llewellyn, are you trying to tell me that you've——'

'Warned him off, yes. Now, do you want to drive down with me?'

'What? . . . No! . . . I——' In a turmoil she swung to the window and gazed unseeingly out across the smooth green slopes but when she heard a movement at the door she turned her head.

'I'm leaving in five minutes,' he told her as their eyes locked briefly. Then he swivelled and went out leaving Storm fuming and wondering just what it was that Carlo had said to make David cancel at such short notice. Still seething, she made her way down to the yard. Of course, she told herself, she could decline his invitation of a lift—and stay at home. But the prospect of sitting by herself with such a violent anger inside her was an unpleasant prospect. Celebration or not, she must find out what it was Carlo had told poor David.

He made no comment when she appeared beside the Rolls, but she was vibrantly conscious of the way his blue eyes roamed her body, lingering longer than they should have where the soft swell of her breasts was cupped by the restraining fabric of her silk bodice.

As he leaned across to help her with her seat belt she could feel the tingle of warmth from his skin and smell the subtle male scent of him mingling with the delicate perfume of the hair-dressing he wore. Blue-black, his hair glowed softly and looked infinitely touchable and despite everything, she felt a pang of love as she focused briefly on the little black hairs that brushed and accentuated his jutting cheekbones.

His lips compressed briefly in a smile as he adjusted the buckle. 'Not too tight, I hope?' His dark-lashed eyes glinted like silver in the deeply tanned face. 'I would hate to crush your—er—dress . . .'

Her chin rose and she gave him a grim look before staring straight ahead. She had wanted to ask him what he meant by saying that he had warned David off, but something about his formidable presence made her quail inside at the prospect of clashing with him now while she was so vulnerably at his mercy within the close confines of his car. The whole cabin seemed to be alive with an electric charge that could set off sparks if they moved any closer. She shrank back in the white leather seat, her face averted, studying the familiar countryside like a traveller in a foreign land.

He drove in silence, his thoughts apparently elsewhere, the distance preserved between them. Yet how she yearned to touch him, to have him touch her, to feel the silky smooth muscles slide demandingly against her own. It was an agony, the power of the sweet desire that went on even when he ushered her out of the car and across the forecourt into the restaurant towards the room that had been specially booked for them all.

Isabella, vibrant as some hot-house flower in scarlet and pink, swooped forward to kiss Carlo effusively on the cheek, then she led him to the head of the table in triumph. Storm would have been only too glad to have slunk into an empty space somewhere out of the limelight, but she found she was being placed on Carlo's right hand, with Isabella on his left. The empty place beside her had been removed and she found she was sitting next to the man who had been in charge of the building work.

'You were rather late, darling,' Isabella reproved, 'but never mind, everyone has been getting to know each other in the cocktail lounge.'

Storm smiled a greeting at Megan, pretty in grey silk, accompanied by her next door neighbour, a widower, and Luce had brought along the much-mentioned Hughie. Bravely Phyllis had brought her ailing brother Dai who had been let out of hospital only the previous week, and he was smiling, though white-faced, and obviously pleased to be back in the swing of things after his long illness. Storm was surprised to see him but she waved to Phyllis, pleased for her after her long months of worry.

There were gales of laughter bursting sporadically from all sides, and Carlo looked down the length of the table with evident enjoyment.

'It seems to be getting off to a good start,' he remarked.

'Yes, you must be feeling very pleased with yourself,' replied Storm cuttingly. She kept her eyes down but felt the strength of his reaction. One hand grasped hers secretly underneath the table. When she lifted her head he didn't say anything but there was a warning gleam in his eyes that made her shudder at the prospect of laying up retribution for herself later on. He let her hand go and turned to speak to someone. His mood was carefree as if now that all the long weeks of work were behind him he could at last relax and be himself. Or, she pondered, was it because he was sitting next to Isabella?—for his eyes turned frequently towards the other woman, plunging daggers of jealousy into Storm's vulnerable heart.

Looking at him now she couldn't believe that his 'special announcement' that Phyllis had mentioned earlier could have anything to do with her after so long had passed and his ridiculous, impulsive proposal had been mentioned no more. His announcement would be something to do with further rewards for the staff—he was obviously adept at keeping everybody happy and working far longer than they would ever want to without the encouragement of his particular brand of blackmail.

'Silent,' he remarked much later when they were half way through the dessert and she had consciously avoided striking up a conversation with him.

'Am I?' She looked at him vaguely through eyes that deliberately focused beyond him, 'I've been having quite an interesting conversation with your builder, actually,' she iced back.

Carlo didn't reply.

Dinner was over and there was dancing to follow on the pocket-sized dance floor with the coloured lights underneath it. Just as Carlo bent his head to her the builder touched her on the arm and asked her to dance with him. Not wanting to hear what Carlo had been about to say, she quickly rose to her feet and followed her stocky little companion out on to the floor. When she sneaked a look back she was surprised to see Carlo standing up, gazing after them with a stunned sort of expression on his face.

The builder, one hand clamped against the small of her back and the other holding her right hand firmly within his own rough one, swirled her into the thick of the crowd—it was only when they rotated past the place where they had been standing that she caught a glimpse of Carlo again. He seemed to be simply standing, gazing out at the dancers. A trick of the light made his face seem pale, pained, haggard almost. The next time she looked he was sitting down, but Isabella was nowhere to be seen. The woman's throaty laugh came from close by and as the builder swung her round in a deftly executed turn, she caught sight of her in the arms of one of Carlo's assistants. The couple were chatting rapidly in Spanish, a fact that gave an air of intimacy to them that made Storm turn her head to see what effect this was having on Carlo.

Obviously not used to being deserted, he was making

no attempt to find a partner and was still gazing blankly into the crowd. Every time she danced past with the builder his eyes would seek out her face, two dark, savage points, boring into her, so that she had consciously to avoid the moment when she anticipated their contact, bending her face to her partner's shoulder, deliberately forcing herself not to glance across to where Carlo was sitting.

The builder was holding her quite possessively now and she had to fight against her instinct to disengage herself from his embrace. A brief glimpse in the mirror that ran down the side of one wall showed her a dancing couple who were enjoying each other's proximity. How deceptive were appearances! By the same token, Carlo himself was in the throes of some violent desolation of the spirit.

The wine and the music and the need to concentrate on the tricky steps the builder insisted on executing didn't manage to drive Carlo from her mind, but it did make it more difficult to keep tabs on him.

She thought she saw him striding rapidly towards the door at one point. Then he reappeared with a succession of partners while she and the builder remained locked in silent contact through an involved sequence of waltzes, quicksteps and disco numbers. Isabella, too, remained with the same partner, and Storm thought it strange that she and Carlo didn't dance together once. His face seemed to show increasing strain; he looked positively murderous by now, and she put it down to his rage at Isabella's behaviour. Obviously her cool aplomb when she caught them in an embrace a few days ago had merely been a façade and she was as angry with him at his infidelity as he obviously was now at her deliberate and public betrayal. There would be fireworks, she judged, before the evening was out.

'My, you're a grand little dancer, Storm. I'm really enjoying this! Makes me feel ten years younger!' the builder said at last, breaking the silence and giving her a friendly look before whirling her out into a flashy foxtrot before she could do more than offer a faint smile in return. She thanked fate that her school had insisted on proper dancing lessons—if she had been less adept the builder would no doubt have abandoned her and she would have been left defenceless at the side of the dance floor with nothing to do but dwell on every turn of Carlo's dark head, and every nuance of the pain that was so plainly etched on his face.

Covertly she watched him even now over her partner's shoulder. His eyes glittered almost black in their deeply shadowed sockets, his skin was pale despite the permanent tan, and he looked almost haggard in the revolving lights that flashed now eerily blue, now green, now satanic red, transforming his expression, so it seemed to her fevered imagination, into a hectic mask of diabolical menace. But she reminded herself, it was nothing to do with her—it was Isabella who would be made to suffer. The thought gave her no comfort though, for it meant that Carlo must be crazily in love with her to be made so visibly wretched at the sight of her dancing with another man.

It was as one number ended and another began that she found herself moving on to the floor next to the object of Carlo's palpable desire. Isabella's left hand was draped casually over her partner's sleeve and it was like a thunderbolt striking down on Storm's head when her glance fell on the large diamond and emerald engagement ring on Isabella's finger. So *that* was the reason for Carlo's almost manic despair! Isabella, his fiancée, was already making up to another man—even though she was now wearing his ring! Rai's words came back to her—'They have had an understanding for years,' he had told her. Well, so much for that! she thought, trembling with a sudden acute stab of compassion for Carlo. No wonder he was looking so murderously angry. For a moment she almost forgot her own pain as she imagined how he must be feeling. It was odd, she thought next, why he didn't go marching up to demand his rights to her loyalty—odd, and strangely out of character.

Isabella was laughing gaily in the arms of the South American, oblivious, it seemed, to Carlo's anguish.

The builder began to lead her towards the bar just then but before they had got very far, she felt a hand on her shoulder. It was rough, not a polite tap by any means, so that she swung round abruptly, losing her partner almost at once in the crowd, so that when a voice hissed in her ear, 'My dance next, I think,' she had no way of excusing herself before Carlo swept her up against the taut, angry muscles of his body. Before she had time to collect her wits she found herself drowning in the syrupy liquid sweetness of a slow waltz. Rivers of emotion seemed to carry her along in his arms. Her limbs seemed to melt into his, and it was only the rock-like face on which were carved deep channels of anguish that made her guess at his arrogant insistence that she should dance with him.

Vengeance was leading him to use her to hurt back at his fiancée in the same way Isabella had chosen to hurt him!

It was an agony and an ecstasy to be in his arms. Shudders of pleasure ran constantly through her body, and she was powerless to resist when she felt his lips brush her neck.

'Oh, Storm!' he murmured huskily into her ear. 'Forgive me, please darling, forgive me . . . I've really blown it, haven't I? I seem to have done everything wrong from the very beginning! I've behaved like a complete fool . . . I'm so sorry, so sorry! Can you ever feel anything for me? Please say it isn't too late.'

Slowly she raised her long-lashed eyes in astonishment to his. If she had yearned to hear any words in all the world it would be these words from this man. Her lips parted slightly, a tear beginning to glisten on her dark ashes. But just at that moment she heard Isabella's seductive laugh beside them and the exotic accent as she exclaimed volubly in Spanish to her partner. Carlo must have been aware of her proximity when he spoke. It was for sure that Isabella had heard his words. Storm felt a violent rush of pain erode her body. It was cruelly easy to see why he had said what he had, even though his voice had been kept to little more than a whisper. To anyone passing his dark head bent to hers in that intimate fashion could suggest only one thing. How the mirrors distorted everything!

Before she could bring any kind of reply to her suddenly dry lips there was a commotion from another part of the floor. She turned in time to see Dai, Phyllis's brother, slowly slide to the floor. The band leader couldn't see that anything was wrong and carried on conducting but the group of dancers slowly swirled to a halt around the motionless form of the man. With an exclamation of concern, Carlo released the enveloping hold he had on Storm and in three strides was bending over him. Unable to grasp what was happening, she was still reeling from the impact Carlo's words had had on her, she watched him clear a path to the edge of the floor. The band at last fell silent and a knot of dancers, staggering under the burden, lifted Dai to the chair someone pulled forward.

Carlo, she noticed in a daze, was slackening Dai's collar, and, with an effortless assumption of authority, he eventually led the way out into the foyer, with willing helpers conveying the now conscious but still obviously unwell man after him.

Still feeling that it was all some kind of nightmarish dream from which she would soon awake, she watched Megan pull Phyllis with her towards the door. A little group of Phyllis and Dai's friends moved off and Isabella came over to Storm.

'My dear, you look shattered. It surely can't have been

as much a shock as all that. Didn't you know he was ill?'

Slowly Storm raised her eyes to those of her rival. She managed only a croaking, non-committal response. Was it a gleam of triumph in Isabella's eyes that she could see? She hated herself for the fact that despite the sudden incident her body was racked uncontrollably by a quite different and personal pain, bereft of the embrace which whether stolen or not, had brought her a few moments of ineffable joy.

Blindly she followed Isabella out into the foyer where the pallor of her face elicited some sympathy, making her feel like a hypocrite—they all assumed it was due to her concern for Dai that she looked so distraught. No one knew it was because her whole life had just been built up into a fantastic copy of paradise to be smashed to pieces only a moment later. She felt close to madness, as if nothing, ever, would make sense again.

Isabella laid a manicured finger on her wrist. 'My dear, you look rather shaken. Can I get you anything?'

She could afford to be kind, thought Storm desperately, for she had won, brilliantly, without even being aware that there had been any contest. Her effect on Carlo was all Storm would ever have wanted—not that she would ever have treated him so cruelly should she have been lucky enough to win his love in the first place. She gave a shaky laugh. 'It was so unexpected,' she stated ambiguously.

Carlo had taken Dai to the hospital in the Rolls, they learned when the others returned. 'I suspect he will be there some time,' observed Isabella to Storm. 'Come, I'll drive you back to Fferllys——'

'N-no, really ... I'll—I'll get a taxi——' Storm protested.

'Nonsense. Carlo would never forgive me. Besides, I have a couple of suitcases in my boot. I may as well stay from tonight as planned.' She raised her sleekly coiffed head. 'Had you forgotten I was supposed to be moving in this weekend?'

Storm trembled convulsively. She hadn't forgotten, of course, but after yesterday it seemed an irrelevance. Now she could see the planning behind it. First the announcement of their engagement, then the sharing of accommodation. Afterwards, no doubt, the wedding. Carlo obviously had little regard for convention. She felt sick. She had fallen for his proposal like a baby. Now it was all the same to her who drove her back home. In time she would learn to school herself to the sight of Carlo and Isabella, to the sound of their names, linked forever by both love and law.

Wildly she plotted escape—the prospect now of staying on at Fferllys was untenable. Better to be jobless, homeless and penniless, now that she had lost her heart too.

Both women were silent as they made their way out to the car park a short time later. Some attempt had been made to get the party going again, but in their hearts everyone was worrying about Dai—in a small community such as theirs, he had been a friend of most of them since schooldays.

Isabella drove fast and efficiently, quite as Storm expected of the woman Carlo would choose, and as the car neared the end of the journey she took her eyes briefly from the road to murmur something about Dai. Then she added, 'Storm, when anything like this happens it always makes me doubly conscious of all the many opportunities we ignore to be truly honest with each other. Life is short and death can catch up on us all, leaving many things undone, regrets for things that should have been said.'

When Storm didn't reply Isabella went on, 'You're a remarkably beautiful child, as well as being very gifted, but I sense a great sadness in you. I would so like us to be friends but something seems to prevent you from liking me—if it's anything that you can talk about, please know that I am always available.'

Storm studied the flickering lights on the dashboard of Isabella's sports car before replying, 'I'm not such a child, you know.' There was a pause.

'From my vantage point, forgive me—at thirty-six . . .' Isabella gave an apologetic chuckle.

Thankfully for Storm they arrived back at the house just then and she scrambled hurriedly out of the car as soon as it pulled up. After making a show of fumbling around in her bag to find the key to the door, she barged inside, saying coldly over her shoulder, 'I suppose you know where you'll be sleeping?'

Without waiting for a reply she began to feel her way upstairs in the dark. One relief, she told herself savagely, the walls were thick—at least there would be no night sounds to jar her 'childish' slumbers.

Scorched by the humiliating thought that Isabella must be speaking for Carlo himself when she dubbed her 'child' she could only throw herself, still fully clothed, onto her bed and succumb to the tears that had been bottled up for what seemed like an eternity.

How pathetic her attempt to look sophisticated in the little black dress seemed now! How Carlo must have been laughing up his sleeve at her, when he already had a relationship with the sleek and sophisticated Isabella. Why had he duped her like this? But she already knew why—he had even warned her of his plan. He must have thought it extremely funny to find that he could turn her on with such ridiculous ease by the mere touch of his cheating lips.

It was agony to learn once and for all that he had merely been amusing himself right from the start with 'the child'—while Isabella, mature and sophisticated was wearing his ring.

In a fever of self-abasement she tried to see it from his point of view. A man of his age—whatever that was—would obviously want someone as experienced as himself. Isabella would fit the bill perfectly, despite the fact that she must be a couple of years older than Carlo. She remembered David's predilection for older women. It was all so clear now. She herself and her anguished love were of no significance to anyone—she was a plaything and it was bitter medicine to realise that this was exactly as Carlo had always treated her.

She burned with the image of his strong-boned face, with the deep lines of experience that would groove into a breath-stopping smile as the blue eyes danced with devilish amusement. The memory taunted her of his hard, strong body moving in passionate contact with her own. 'Carlo,' she moaned helplessly, gripping her pillow in both hands and burying her tear-stained face in its comforting softness. He had got his revenge now, ten times over. He had reduced her to a quivering mass of pain just as he had threatened he would.

Stiffly she climbed off the bed and began to pull undone the crumpled black dress. How silly her fantasies seemed now—his strong brown fingers would never unbutton her dress with that slow, sensual delight she longed to experience. She would never feel the heated power of that beloved body take her to the edge of paradise and beyond.

She hurled the dress across the room. It was over. Tomorrow she would start to look for somewhere else to live.

So lost was she in the misery of her pain that she didn't hear the light tap on her door, and only when it began to open did she spin in alarm, dashing a hand across her tear-stained cheeks to hide her grief from the woman who had unwittingly caused it all.

Then she gasped, for it wasn't Isabella who stood there, framed in the doorway, but Carlo himself. 'I—I didn't hear the car,' she blurted.

'You got back all right? I was worried—— '

'Isabella brought me. She's no doubt waiting for you in your room——' She was going to go on to pour out all her hurt in a burst of recriminations, but something about the look on his face made her stop.

He came slowly into the room. His eyes had darkened and with a shudder of guilt she remembered Dai and before she could ask Carlo anticipated her question. 'It's not good,' he told her. 'They're going to keep us informed. I've had the phone put through to my room. Phyllis is staying at Megan's tonight.'

He moved aimlessly about, pausing when he saw the dress in a crumpled heap in a corner of the room. 'Do you always throw your clothes down like that?' he asked, raising his dark head quizzically to her. 'We'll have to have a rule about it. I prefer order myself.'

'I'll do as I like in my own room,' she told him with quivering lips.

'In your own room, yes, but what happens when you share mine?'

'Is that likely?' she demanded scornfully, her lips beginning to tremble, amazed that even now he could taunt her with the lie that they had a future together.

'Storm, please . . . is it really too late for us? I can't make myself believe it. Feelings like this must mean something. You're driving me crazy—do you know that?' As he came towards her she was acutely conscious all of a sudden that she was wearing nothing but bra and pants and she hastily grabbed a towelling robe and pulled it on. His eyes followed her movements, dark pain visible in their depths.

'Why do you go on talking like this to me, Carlo?' she demanded stiffly.

'I want you, Storm. I'm crazy about you. I'll give you anything you want, everything I have. What more can I say to convince you?'

'Stop it!' she cried brokenly, clamping both hands tightly over her ears. 'I won't hear it! I won't! Go away! Leave me in peace! Please Carlo . . .' There was a sob in her voice. 'Get out of my life!'

He put out a hand as if to force her to listen to him and her whole body fired up with a frustration of longing to feel his touch on her skin, but she fought the desire with a savagery she didn't know she possessed.

'Don't touch me!' she ground hoarsely, stepping back out of reach.

His eyes shone luminous, black as ice, and his face paled. A battle seemed to take place deep in his soul and a look of bewilderment touched his face. Then he shrugged and his eyes became cold slits. 'Still fighting me? Why Storm? Why?'

When she didn't answer he shrugged again, wearily, like a man on the brink of total defeat.

'Maybe we'll see things more clearly in the morning. Let's talk properly then. Get some sleep now.' He made for the door and when he turned his eyes were full of anguish. 'Please, Storm, think things over. Let's make a fresh start, wipe out all the mistakes of the past. Don't throw our love away, please, Storm, don't throw it away.'

The door closed on the sound of her bitter laughter. Love? What was he talking about? He didn't love her. He lusted for her. He had admitted as much. Now he was trying yet another ploy to get her into his bed. The man was a consummate actor—that look of pain on his face would have fooled her if she hadn't caught sight of Isabella's ring. Did he think she was stupid or something? How could she wipe out all the mistakes and start again? How could she, dear God, how could she when he had hurt her so much? And how could he possibly suggest she forget the past when he was engaged to someone else—and was systematically and coldly setting out to savage her soul to death?

She lay all night like a block of wood between the cold sheets with her eyes staring blankly into the dark. By morning she had come to the decision that it would be the last night she would ever spend at Fferllys.

CHAPTER TEN

IT was not so easy to put her resolution into practice, for, despite her desperate longing to escape from the web of pain that the presence of Carlo and his fiancée represented, in the cold light of morning she knew she couldn't simply walk out on her obligations to Megan and the others. It would be the same as putting them all out of a job, and that was the very thing she had striven to avoid ever since David's bombshell announcement of the will.

Nor was she keen to concede victory to Carlo—by being forced out she would be playing into his hands—and hadn't he told her at the beginning that she couldn't win and may as well give in straight away? Her defiant warning that he had better prepare himself for defeat rang hollowly now, but she had sufficient spirit left to want to stand her ground to the bitter end.

No, rather than run away, she would stay and try to find a way of running the business down gradually. There was nothing to stop her trying to find premises elsewhere. This was something she had thought of at the beginning but had then allowed her judgment to be clouded by events. It was a foolish mistake, she told herself as she showered and dressed, hoping that if she relegated it to the realm of decisions that should not have been made she could exorcise some of the power Carlo held over her.

Everyone seemed understandably subdued when they arrived for work. Storm had eaten only the skimpiest breakfast in fear of bumping into Carlo and Isabella and had already set out the morning's work when they came straggling up the lane. Phyllis was staying at the hospital all day—Dai's condition was unchanged—and with one less hand in the printing workshop they were going to be hard-pressed to complete their current batch of work. On top of that, with it being Saturday, they would be finishing early anyway.

Megan stopped by the printing table as Storm mixed up some new colours for the next batch of fabric and gave her a rather searching look. 'Forgive me for saying this, Storm, but you look dreadful. Are you feeling all right?'

'I didn't sleep much last night,' she admitted, keeping her head bent.

'You didn't seem too good at dinner actually—I was going to ask you what was up, but what with poor Dai and that, I didn't get the chance.' She patted her shoulder. 'You've had a lot on your plate since Bronwen's accident. I don't think you've properly got over it. You ought to take things steady for a while. Carlo's going to help with the business side a bit, isn't he?'

'Not if *I* can help it,' she burst out.

Megan looked nonplussed. 'I'm sorry—I must have misunderstood—I thought that's what he said?'

'What he says he's going to do and what he actually does are not necessarily the same thing, as it happens.' Her tone was so unexpectedly bitter that Megan took a step back but she had a thoughtful look in her eyes when she said, 'I can understand how you must have felt in the beginning,' her voice was gentle, 'but I think he's turned out to be a real stroke of luck for us all.'

'Yes, hasn't he just!' Storm was sarcastic. 'As far as I'm concerned he's been an unmitigated disaster and he can go to hell—the last thing I want is Mr High-and-Mighty Llewellyn poking his nasty prying fingers in my affairs, and as soon as I can find a suitable alternative I'm going to move the whole works out from Fferllys lock, stock and barrel! And if you or any of the others get a better offer from his lordship you're welcome to take it. I've had as much as I can take from——'

Something about Megan's expression made Storm's

words trail off into silence. She knew, even before she turned to the door, that Carlo would be standing with his lean length casually propped in it. She turned. He was.

'Good,' she clipped when she saw him.

A silence wrapped everybody in it and they were all suddenly very busy with what they were doing.

'I'm so glad you decided to eavesdrop, Carlo. At least I won't have to repeat what I've just told Megan.' Somehow or other she managed to force a smile, brilliant because of the sheen of hurt and angry tears that battled beneath her lids, to show how little she really cared.

His face seemed ashen and for once there was no immediate verbal come-back, he merely stared at her, eyes boring into hers as if trying to read off some hidden message in her expression.

'You have a great sense of timing, don't you, Carlo? I really ought to congratulate you,' she went on, forcing herself to go on talking in order to stave off the sudden, unnerving power of his silence. What was the matter with him? Why was he staring at her like that? Did he seriously expect her to go on being humiliated by the continual sight and sound of him now that he was marrying someone else?

With her defences suddenly crumbling around her, she hurled the rubber squeegee across the workshop, where it landed in a spatter of purple dye at his feet, then with a suffocating coil of rage, she sprang across towards the door, pushing violently past him with a gritted, 'Get out of my way!' before she started to run and run, tears boiling down her pale cheeks, until she came to the road outside the gates.

Once outside she left the public road straight away and set out upon the winding sheep track that led up to the summit of Pen-y-Llyn. She kept on climbing until she was breathless and the cold wind had dried the tears on her cheeks. Even then she forced herself to climb higher until Fferllys itself was just a jumble of grey walls in a curve of the hill.

When she came to the cliff escarpment at the summit she flung herself down and gazed for a long time at the landscape folding away into the distance. Bronwen's voice saying, 'There's nothing like a mountain top for giving you a perspective on things,' came back to her, and she tried to make herself believe in the littleness of love and the fleeting pleasure of one man's touch, but the pain was too close, too recent, and she could only suffer numbly, praying that the passage of time would eventually bring with it the healing of all wounds.

It was a spring day with the sun warm and the lambs about, but as she had climbed the air had become thinner and sharper and she regretted that she had let him drive her out without a coat. She began to shiver in her thin blouse and jersey, but she could not go back, she decided. She would rather die than go back and face them all. Let her see the women walking back down the lane to the village. Let her see them all go, then she would return. By the time Monday came around the whole scene would be half-forgotten. And she would lock her door at nights—to keep him out and possibly herself in—until she had plotted her escape.

At least he knew now how things were going to be for ever more between them.

The great mountain wilderness spread far away to the south to the foot of Plynlimon, covering many hundreds of square miles of crag and torrent. There were hidden becks up here and hills covered in bogs that were like bottomless pits, lidded over by a bright green crust and as supportive of the unwary walker as blancmange. There were hundred-foot precipices that looked like bits of rock flung down by a giant hand, and pools as blue-black as the darkest eyes she had ever looked into. She loved the mountain, its wildness, its unpredictable changes, its multi-coloured variety when the sun shone, even its treacherous face half-hidden in mist, but she knew she couldn't stay up here forever.

Then she gave a start of fright as loose stones rattled noisily over the rocks. A man's dark head came into view as he climbed rapidly hand over hand across the escarpment on whose brim she sat.

'You've had most of the morning in which to cool down. Here—you'll no doubt need this by now.' He thrust a thick woollen jacket into her hands, despite her protests, then, sitting down beside her, opened a bag that had been slung over his shoulder and began to take out a flask and some sandwiches and a few pieces of fruit. She watched him in astonishment and when he offered her a drink from the flask she burst out, 'What do you think this is? It's my life—not a weekend picnic!'

'Oh, come on, you must be frozen and hungry. You've been sitting up here in this wind for hours.'

'How do you know?'

'I've been watching you from the house.'

'Haven't you anything better to do than spy on me?'

'I can't think of anything, no.'

A betraying impulse to believe him made her turn her head in pain. Even now she was defenceless against his hurtful manipulation of her feeling, his smooth flattery that weakened all her resistance to him.

'I could push you off this rock as easily as anything,' she told him tightly, staring fixedly at the tiled roofs of the house far below.

'You could,' he agreed. 'Do you want to?'

'Yes.'

'Liar.'

She spun in fury at being goaded, knowing he was right, and as her hand lifted he caught it effortlessly in mid air then held it firmly between his own two strong hands even as she tried to wriggle free. He began to stroke it thoughtfully, looking at her all the time through slitted, watchful eyes that made her squirm with the desire to go—to stay, to be in his arms forever.

Her cheeks flushed hotly. 'Don't stare at me like that.'

'I'm going to tell you a story.' He squeezed her hand to still her. 'See the forest down below?'

Automatically she glanced to the sea of variegated green that stretched from the head of the valley to the horizon.

'What about it?' she asked sulkily, aching with the pain that these sudden few unexpected minutes alone might be the last they would ever spend together.

'One night in winter, long ago,' he began, 'it started to rain . . .'

'I'm not a child,' she told him fiercely.

'Never mind, just listen—now, it didn't just rain, a few drops then stop—it poured down, ceaselessly, all night long. It was so cold, that night, that the rain froze as it fell and everything it touched was coated with ice. Every blade of grass, every twig, every branch of every tree was wrapped deep in a sheath of transparent ice.'

He's treating me like a child, she thought bitterly, beginning to listen despite herself.

'To those who saw it, they said it took some of the light from the moonlit sky and reflected it back from a thousand surfaces so that everything gleamed and glittered and shone like glass.'

Her large violet eyes were misty with emotion as she helplessly succumbed to the magic of his voice—there was a seductive Welsh lilt to it that she had never properly listened to before and for the first time she recognised the wildness of his Welsh blood that was like a lyrical counterpoint to the fire of his Spanish ancestors.

'Shall I go on?' he murmured, noting her stillness. Her hand was still clasped in his. She could feel the pulse of the blood in his veins as her warmth mingled with his, and when he put his other arm around her shoulders and drew her close she had no will to resist. It was all for one last time, she told herself, this memory would have to last for ever.

'Please do,' she whispered, huddling against him.

'Well,' he continued quietly, 'under the unexpected burden of the ice, branches from the trees began to bend and when a slight wind arose the branches began to snap off and fall with a sound like the far off shattering of crockery. It was a strange, magical sound, and the people in Fferllys listened to it throughout the night, not knowing what it was.' He paused. 'In the morning when they went to the windows and looked out they saw a scene of desolation—the beautiful larches of the forest, and the firs and the brittle ash trees had had their branches snapped off by the ice—and the people knew then that all night long they had been listening to the death agonies of the trees. Their branches lay in heaps around them like shed garments,' he paused again. 'Next day my father left Fferllys and returned to South America to his wife . . . I think that was maybe the last time he and Bronwen were together.'

Storm had a lump in her throat for the way her imagination conveyed with heart-breaking clarity the anguish Bronwen must have suffered as she kissed her lover goodbye, knowing, perhaps, that it would be for ever. Tears rained silently down her cheeks, soaking into the dark wool of Carlo's sweater.

'I heard that story first from my father,' he told her quietly, 'though of course he didn't name the people in it. And I read it again just now in your aunt's diary. Forgive me, Storm, I had to find out what she was really like.'

Her head was still bent into the protective hollow of his chest.

'Storm?'

'It's all right, she wouldn't have minded . . . She never denied your father anything so I'm sure she wouldn't mind if his son—even though your mother——' She broke off, the words blocked by the lump in her throat.

'Last time I was home,' he continued, 'I had a talk to Mother about Bronwen. I thought it was time everything came out into the open. There had been hints enough that she had done everything she could to hang on to Father. She's a determined woman and she was positive she was not going to let Father go without ruining him in any way she could. His response was simply to retreat into his books, his fantasies. It has made me realise that I wronged Bronwen. She wasn't the sort of woman I thought she was.'

He went on, 'I could only look back to that time when there had been such dreadful fights over this other woman—I didn't know that it had been as unexpected and painful for her as for anyone else. I was bitterly resentful that Father could betray my mother and I didn't know that it was Bronwen who had refused to continue the affair when she discovered what was involved. It was Bronwen who urged him to return to his wife, and it was Father who let it overshadow his whole life after that. But then,' he laughed bitterly, 'she was like you, wasn't she, Storm? So how could he help it? . . . Even when I was a child I used to think of her as the Welsh witch Ceridwen, weaving her spells—and maybe it's not so far from the truth after all?'

He tilted her face up to his own. Their lips were almost touching but Storm tried to draw back.

I'm not your enemy any longer, Storm. Please try not to see me as a hated intruder. I'll make it up to you if you'll let me.'

Storm felt a cold power strip her to nakedness. He was going to marry another woman, yet he could make love to her with such skilled flattery that she was almost ready to give in. If she dropped her defences again he would trap her with the silken promises of his wicked Welsh tongue until she meekly handed over her life to him. If his motive was no longer to avenge the past, his goal was still the same, to possess and corrupt her.

Wildly she scrambled to her feet, slithering a little on the wind-carved rock.

'I'm going down now, Carlo——'

'Wait!' He looked bewildered.

'It's all right. You don't have to say any more. I understand what a shock it must be for you to discover that Bronwen wasn't the scarlet woman you so fondly imagined. But anyone can make mistakes.' She looked down at him from her vantage point higher up the rock. 'You mustn't blame yourself. Even the best of us jump to conclusions some time. Now I really must go——'

Blinded by sudden tears she half-turned to leave. His shout of warning came too late and with a little gasp she found herself falling headlong over a jutting rock, then she was rolling helplessly over the springy turf, finally coming to rest in a hollow between two rocks.

In a trice he was kneeling beside her. 'Dear God, you're not safe to be let out alone,' he murmured, pulling her into the circle of his arms where she could hear the rapid drumming of his heart against her ribs. 'What would have happened if you'd fallen the other way?'

'I'd be dead,' she observed with gloomy satisfaction.

'You little idiot.' He hugged her to him, fondling her head roughly in his two large hands. 'Lesson one, don't play games on cliff edges.'

She began to laugh hysterically. 'But that's exactly what I've been doing ever since you arrived here and——' She bit back the words that would betray the depth of her feelings and correcting herself added shortly, 'Children are supposed to play games, aren't they?'

'Please don't play them with me.'

'It has to be all one way, of course—you play games and make all the rules too.'

'I wish I could—you need a few rules, you've run wild for too long.'

He was holding her again, crooked in the arch of his body so that they were lying on the soft turf in the shelter of the rocks and in a private world where only the egg-shell blue of the sky curved over them. He became aware of the seclusion of the spot just as she did.

'Alone at last.'

'No, Carlo——' Her violet eyes darkened in panic.

'Why no? Your body says yes, and I've waited so long—oh, Storm, hasn't anything I've said meant a thing to you? I admit my mistakes—but when I first met you I had to fight against what my instincts were telling me. Even if Bronwen had had a hundred lovers and you were following in her footsteps, you were still totally desirable. But I couldn't admit that, even to myself. I had to pretend I was avenging my mother's lost honour—of course it wasn't lost at all—she has the life she wanted, running the family business. Don't you see?'

'Yes, yes.' She moved, trying to ease her throbbing body away from the source of its craving.

'So why can't you forgive me?'

'You have to ask . . .?' She stared at him stupidly. 'You want to take everything from me! I can't forgive that!' Her eyes flashed, yet she was so near to giving in to him that she had to close them to shut out the sight of the face whose every line she would remember for ever. Nothing, it seemed, would make him stop trying to goad her into giving him all she had, but he was too dangerous to love. The lightest touch of his finger down the side of her face sent a spasm of pleasure through her whole body even though she knew it was a simple, calculated move by an arch-seducer. He wanted her, he wanted her, but they were more alike than he knew, for she too wanted everything—she wanted his love-making, yes, but she wanted his smile, his touch, and she wanted his companionship and his conversation, but above all that she wanted the one thing he wouldn't give her because he would have to give that to the woman who became his wife—she wanted his love.

Already his hands were twining in her hair, sending little quivers of excitement rushing through her veins. One hand unerringly found a way underneath her blouse and she was helpless against the tiny shivers of response at the touch of his fingers as he caressed the smooth, satiny skin, stroking it gently, provokingly, until he found the rounded shape of her breast, sending darts of pleasure at the touch. Then she heard the soft whisper as he spoke her name and the sensation of his touch was so arousing she began to give small moans of pleasure, letting her neck arch to receive the tantalising pressure of his lips in hot waves of mounting torment.

Something more powerful than the need to protect herself from him stirred inside her like some blind atavistic urge that was an emanation of the weeks of pain and longing that had kept him in the forefront of her mind, and, all the promises she had made to herself forgotten, she lifted up her lips to his so that her name was torn from him in a harsh cry of desire as his lips came down to claim hers, biting urgently into the soft flesh of her tongue, sliding deep into the recesses of her throat as he brought her to the shuddering threshold of desire.

She clung in despair to the body of the man she loved as he began to arch over her but when he began to fumble at the buckle of her jeans and the cold mountain air struck the tender warmth of her exposed flesh she gave a shudder of fright and tried to claw at the strong back pinning her hips to the soft grass.

'No, Carlo—please don't——' she moaned, torn by wanting *and* loving a man who only wanted but did not love her.

'You want me, Storm, so why not go on?'

'You don't care about me, Carlo,' she mumbled, overcome with longing and even now succumbing to the ragged caresses that were inciting her to abandon herself totally to his hunger.

'I care, my lovely child, of course I care,' he murmured thickly, jerking his head back in surprise as the word 'child' brought her fingers raking painfully through the thick, dark hair in a spasm of aching memory.

His first lazy and insulting words to her had been to call her child as he bade her to go and fetch the grown-ups on the day he had made his first appearance at Fferllys. How could she now have lost herself so far as to forget that that was all she would ever be to him?

Driven by despair she began to kick out with her legs against the pinioning of his body, raking the nails of one hand down the side of his cheek, destroying all the languor aroused by the magic of his touch in the catapulting of an anger that sent her arching against him like a wild cat.

With a start of surprise his hands automatically came up to defend himself, yanking her head back by the hair and pinning her writhing limbs roughly to the ground in one savage movement.

'I get the message! "No" means "no." But why the sudden change of mood? What have I done? What have I said?'

'Let me go!' she cried hoarsely, jerking her head from side to side in a fever to get away. The black lashes came down, veiling his eyes, and she saw the clean-cut jaw clench in a spasm of emotion. With a shock she felt him roll away from her and stand up, his back to the sun.

'Get up! I'll see you safely down the slope.' He thrust out a hand and yanked her to her feet, brushed some leaves of wild grass roughly from where they stuck to her jacket and began to drag her back down the mountain-side. He descended at such a pace it was all she could do to keep up with him and she felt herself slipping and sliding, saved from crashing to her knees only by the cruel grip by which he held her.

Before they got within earshot of the house he stopped abruptly and swung round to face her and in a raw voice told her, 'That was clear enough, Storm. I don't think I need telling again. I can't guess what little game you're playing—I wanted to give you everything, but you'd obviously prefer to drink poison than have me. I'm not going to scar myself wondering why. You're right in one thing—it'd be best if you left as soon as possible. I'll do what I can to find you another workshop in one of the nearby towns if that's what you want. In the meantime, just keep the hell out of my way!'

The words seemed ripped from his throat and she told herself that this was what happened when a man was aroused to such a lust of wanting and then frustrated at the last moment. She hadn't meant it to happen, but she had been unable to help herself. It was as much his fault as her own. He shouldn't have arrogantly assumed she was just going to drop into his lap like a ripe apple.

She watched him stride rapidly down the rest of the path and after giving him a minute or two to get ahead, she followed more slowly, her heart like the dead weight of a block of arctic ice.

She knew all about the 'everything' he wanted to give her—Bronwen had shown her what sort of poisoned gift that could turn out to be. She was lucky she had been able to fight him off in time. It wasn't even really her he wanted, it all came down to the simple masculine need tc dominate.

Isabella was walking to her car as Storm came in through the arch and when she caught sight of her she checkec and came towards her with a puzzled frown that didn't quite manage to conceal the jaunty air of high spirits that seemed to surround her. 'What on earth's happenec between you two?' she demanded as soon as she was within earshot, taking in Storm's white face and se expression.

Storm tried to brush past. She knew she would start tc sob hysterically out here in front of this torturing womar if she couldn't get upstairs into the privacy of her owr room at once.

'Storm!' She felt Isabella tug at her arm, but already scalding tears were lashing her cheeks and she stumbled trying to shake off the restraining hand.

'Storm, look, I can't stop now. I'm going down to meet my fiancé at the station, but when I come back we'll talk.'

Storm's held breath ached before she thought to let it out. 'What?' she croaked.

'Let me talk to you when I come back. I'll only be gone half an hour.' She peered kindly into Storm's face. 'Are you sure you're all right. I really must dash. His train's due in fifteen minutes.'

With a little wave of her hand that set the jewels sparkling on her ring finger she ran lightly across to her car and climbed in.

Storm, still breathing raggedly, watched as she drove rapidly out of the courtyard with a friendly wave of her hand. She was still standing there when she saw Carlo coming out of the house carrying a suitcase. She watched, too stunned to move, as he stowed it in the boot of the Rolls. When he went back into the house again she was moved to action.

'Carlo!' she screeched, throwing herself headlong across the cobblestones, nearly colliding with him as he came out carrying a jacket and a bunch of keys.

He sprang back as if burned and for a minute their eyes locked, tuned to a powerful current that united them despite what had passed between them before.

'What are you doing?' she demanded hoarsely. 'Where are you going?'

'I'm getting out. Have Fferllys! Take it all, with my best wishes!' he told her savagely. 'You win, Storm. I'm not fighting any more.'

'But you can't go! You can't!' She flung herself against him, hugging him against her, frightened by the way his body recoiled away from hers and his expression turned even more grim than before.

'I thought you were going to marry Isabella——' she told him brokenly. 'I thought that you and she——' Voice raw with pain, she clung wildly to him, willing him to unbend to her.

'Isabella?' he stared at her with a look of astonishment on his face. 'What made you think that?' he asked huskily. 'I thought you knew she's only like a sister to me? We were brought up together—why did you think that?'

'I noticed her engagement ring—I thought you had given it to her. You were in such a towering rage over something—then you said all those unexpected things just as Dai collapsed . . .'

'So that's why—just now—but I was in a rage because of you, dancing every dance with my builder and apparently enjoying every minute. I thought I'd lost you completely then. And as for Isabella—she's been secretly engaged to my best friend Marco for months—we guessed everybody was speculating about us, but I didn't suspect the rumour had reached you——'

He fumbled towards her, reaching out blindly to fold her roughly into his arms. 'It's you I love,' he told her raggedly. 'I always have.' His hands raked possessively through her hair. 'Ever since I saw you come bursting into the room in that disreputable looking smock, with paint all over your face and looking as if you could spi flames—I was lost from that very moment.'

'Say it to me, Carlo. Say you mean it,' she pleaded, he voice thickening, scarcely daring, even now, to believe what he was telling her. 'More than just wanting— loving? Real love?'

'Real, everlasting, ever-loving, honest-to-goodness love, yes, Storm, all that. Is it so unbelievable?'

'I didn't guess . . . I thought—I thought you onl wanted to seduce me, to hurt me for what you though Bronwen had done.'

His fingers touched her face softly, exploring ever curve of it as if not sure whether she was real or not.

'Yes, I thought I wanted to hurt you, for being s beautiful and desirable and untouchable. I told myself wanted to be able to dismiss you from my life as callously as I thought Bronwen had played with the affections of my father . . .' He bent his head, kissing the side of her neck and leaving a trail of pure bliss as he did so. 'But when I came to carry out my threat everything went wrong and I realised I was deceiving myself if I thought I was immune to you . . . I love you, Storm. I'm crazy about you. Why do you think I changed my mind about letting you stay on at Fferllys? I knew even then that I could never let you go. I had to think of some way of making you stay. Now all I want is to care for you for the rest of my days . . .'

There was a long pause while they looked into each other's eyes, then, as if some wordless message had passed between them he started to lead her inside the empty house. The car with its boot gaping open was abandoned in the middle of the yard, his jacket was dropped carelessly on to the stairs, and, entwined in each other's arms, they slowly began to ascend to the upper floor.

Pausing outside her bedroom, he gazed hungrily into the hazy depths of her eyes and told her resonantly, 'This may be your last chance to say no, my love.' His breath was uneven as he waited for her answer but when it came, it was everything he could have wished for she wordlessly stretched up on tiptoe and pulled his dark head down to her own moist and waiting lips.

'My own love, my lovely Storm. I've been through hell wanting you,' he breathed raggedly as he pushed open the door so that they could enter the room together, his mouth no longer teasing now but pulsing urgently as it covered hers in a fever of possession.

'I was frightened by the way you could make me desire you so easily,' she told him hoarsely as they moved slowly towards the bed. 'It was torture to come anywhere near you——' She was whispering heatedly between his kisses, pouring out all the weeks of pain and misunderstanding and confusion.

'Torture for you?' he murmured huskily as his hands cupped her breasts, deliberately arousing her to a greater torment of longing with the long, sure strokes of his hands over her pearly skin.

'And then when you said it was nothing but lust, dismissing me—what I felt—as if it meant nothing . . .' She shuddered with pleasure as her body began to move hungrily against his, unchecked now by any fear that he would abandon her once he had taken his pleasure, murmuring, 'I couldn't bear the thought that you were deliberately trying to make me yield, that you even used marriage as a threat to make me suffer. I didn't know how you could say you were going to marry me when you seemed to hate me so much——'

'I thought if I married you I would be able to show you what real love meant, that I would be able to teach you that it could be something more than just an expression of physical desire. I thought I was setting out to reform you. At least—that's how I made it acceptable to myself. Really I was just terrified of losing you.' His words were becoming muffled by the kisses he was bestowing on the rosy peaks of her breasts, sensitising every nerve-ending, searching out every vulnerable curve of her body as she abandoned herself to the wild possession of his caresses.

With a sigh of pleasure she felt herself pressed back on to the bed as, his arousal obvious even to her inexperienced eye, he covered her body with his own, their clothes falling away at his touch till they were both naked together at last.

His eyes licked like blue flame over her nakedness as she abandoned herself trustingly to the tender invasion of his touch, yearning to experience what she had never felt before, to do whatever he wanted, to play any role he imposed, helplessly and willingly under his control. But she had to tell him how she had once felt, why she had resisted him in the past.

'I couldn't bear to think of you marrying Isabella—you deliberately taunted me by making me think you were having an affair——'

'I was desperate by that time,' he explained thickly. 'You seemed to want me but you seemed to have no feelings—I wanted to make you jealous, to feel something, anything—to punish you for making me so frantically jealous of David and Rai——'

'I admit I tried to make myself believe I really wanted David, the quiet life——'

'You? . . . yes, I should have known how ridiculous that was. It was only when I spoke to him last night that I realised he could only ever let himself get serious about you if you changed radically, and I knew you wouldn't—Storm by name and Storm by nature he called you——'

His hands skimmed her unexplored body, schooling its paroxysms of ecstasy to the rhythms of his own movements, then his lips covered her own, slowly probing her burning mouth with the soft pressure of his tongue, whipping her emotions to a frenzied pitch, moulding his pulsing body against her own again and again so that she moaned in pleasure beneath him. But he too needed to explain.

'As for Rai—' he told her huskily, raising his head, 'he confessed that you'd given him no encouragement. He simply can't resist a pretty face. He was glad when I told him to go back home to his wife out of temptation's way.'

His voice became inaudible as with mounting excitement he heard her hoarse cry of pleasure as their bodies began to move feverishly together and her responses told him that at last she was offering herself freely, willingly, in all the joy of giving. Explanations came to an end as, limbs entwined without restraint at last, their cries of ecstasy mingled and resounded throughout the house.

Long afterwards he held her in the strong arc of his body,

safe, protected, loved, and she knew she would never need to fear the torment of his dark revenge again, for it had dissolved like a bitter dream in the daylight clarity of their love.

He ran sensitive fingers over the smooth satin of her stomach, telling her with a lopsided smile, 'The past is over—we are both free of it now and I want to marry you for no other reason but love.'

'Tell me again and again—never stop telling me, Carlo,' she murmured contentedly against the smooth skin of his throat.

'I love you, Storm, and only you.'

His mouth moved hotly through her tangled hair as he added, 'The old man knew something after all—I've found the one woman worth walking through fire for.'

As she heard this she was overwhelmed by the feeling that destiny had been fulfilled, love had come full circle to Fferllys, and once again she let him take her lips in the sure knowledge he would never again inflict unwitting hurt on her, and that together their nights would fill the house with the many whispers and cries of true love.

Harlequin Presents

What the press says about Harlequin romance fiction...

"When it comes to romantic novels...
Harlequin is the indisputable king."

—*New York Times*

"...always with an upbeat, happy ending."

—*San Francisco Chronicle*

"Women have come to trust these stories about contemporary people, set in exciting foreign places."

—*Best Sellers*, New York

"The most popular reading matter of American women today."

—*Detroit News*

"...a work of art."

—*Globe & Mail*, Toronto